The Toff and the
Sleepy Cowboy

JOHN CREASEY

The Toff and the Sleepy Cowboy

The 56th Book of the Toff

WALKER AND COMPANY
New York

VS—R.Mcc BA JH

First published in the United States of America in 1975 by
the Walker Publishing Company, Inc.
Published simultaneously in Canada by
Fitzhenry & Whiteside, Limited, Toronto.

ISBN: 0-8027-5313-2

Library of Congress Catalog Card Number: 74-21731

Printed in the United States of America.

10 9 8 7 6 5 4 3 2 1

Contents

c, 1

I

The Man Who Did Not Move

OUT OF THE WARM skies of Arizona in the American great
south-west came a huge aircraft; it flew over high mountains and wide rivers and huge lakes, over deep valleys
where little grew, and over the lush green of the eastern
states until it landed at New York's Kennedy Airport,
after flying over sea and houses, beaches and man-made
lagoons.

All of this took some five hours.

Some of the passengers were tense and apprehensive
before the wheels touched down, others were so used to
air travel that they chafed only at the need to keep their
seat belts fastened. The tension and the impatience van-
ished as the great machine taxied towards the gate which
would lead its passengers to the airport building. The
stewardesses pleaded for them to keep their seats until the
aircraft stopped, and all did. But as the motion ceased it
seemed as if every man and woman present leapt up,
grabbed coats and hats and bags and tried to get into the
gangway first.

In fact, a few, the wise ones, stayed in their seats,
knowing that all would have to wait together until the
baggage was brought from the bowels of the aircraft and
placed on a slow-moving conveyor belt for passengers or
porters to pluck it off. Fewer, elderly or infirm, waited

until the crush was over and stewardesses and kindly fellow-passengers could help.

At last, only one passenger remained in his seat: a man.

He sat upright, his seat belt still fastened, but his chin nestled on his chest.

He appeared to be asleep; certainly he did not move.

For the steward and the stewardesses it had been a trying flight, for bumpiness over the great plains had made some passengers sick and others bad-tempered. The young man who did not move, however, had been a model passenger, hardly seen and seldom heard, and obediently keeping his seat belt fastened during the turbulence. Perhaps that was why he had been overlooked. Two stewardesses, coming from the front of the aircraft, neat-looking, nice-looking, picking up some odds and ends of equipment and magazines from the seats, saw him at the same moment.

"For heavens sakes," exclaimed one, a brunette.

"Some people can sleep through an earthquake," remarked the other, who was a vivid blonde.

The brunette leaned across and touched the young man's arm.

"Excuse me," she said, "but we're in New York."

The young man did not respond in any way.

"Sir, we're in New York." The girl's voice rose.

"We're at Kennedy!" called the fair one, as if that announcement was enough to awaken the dead.

Still the young man did not stir.

"Betty — " the dark-haired girl began.

"Pauline — " began the other.

"You don't think — "

"He can't be!"

Suddenly, these two young women, used to every conceivable emergency in the air, were alarmed. The fair-haired one, also the prettier, went behind the passenger, gripped his shoulders and shook him, but had no effect at all.

"Wake up!" she cried in desperation.

At the front exit two or three men and another stewardess had gathered, laughing and joking as crews often do at the end of a flight. One man, tall, good-looking, peaked cap on the back of his head, noticed the two stewardesses' concern and came along the gangway towards them. He was the captain, and technically responsible for what happened until the machine was handed over to the maintenance men for its check.

"Hi, there," he called, half-way from the exit to the girls. "What's going on?"

One girl turned to look at him, the other had only to raise her head. The dark-haired one answered.

"This passenger won't wake up."

"The flight must have exhausted him," quipped the pilot. "Let me try." He squeezed into the row of seats in front of the sleeping man and tilted his head backwards to reveal a long, bony face, a long, spade of a chin, a high forehead, a long nose with nostrils which had a distended look — and eyelids drawn, tight as shutters, over the large eyes.

It was an unusual face; the kind one did not easily forget.

The skin was tanned deeper than gold. The hair was cut short, making a kind of halo so fair it was like the stubble of corn. The pilot held the head up and gripped the man's shoulder with his free hand, shaking it.

"Hey, there. Wake up, fella!"

The head bobbed under the shaking but there was no other movement.

The pilot's expression changed, as if a shadow of apprehension fell upon him also, and he glanced from girl to girl. To his credit he did not utter the suspicion which had come into his mind, but looked round and called to the men at the front:

"Hey, fellas! We've got a sleeping beauty here. Come and take a look."

They came . . .

Very soon a doctor arrived from the airport, for crews had to use extreme care when a passenger was unwell, and the certain thing now was that this young man was not simply asleep. He was unconscious, with a sluggish pulse. Strictly speaking, the pilot and the stewardesses could have gone off duty, after they had made their reports, but none of them did. Instead, as the passenger was wheeled on a surgical trolley away from the aircraft and by devious routes to the hospital — devious to make sure no other passenger saw him — the captain said:

"Come on girls, I'll buy you a dinner. When we're through we should know what's going on."

"Do you — do you think he's dead?" asked the brunette.

"Could it be something he ate on the aircraft?" asked the fair girl, fearfully.

"What a thing to say before dinner," protested the pilot. He put an arm about each girl and led the way towards the restaurant. "Come on, forget it! He looked good and healthy to me."

As they entered the restaurant, with its soft lights and sparkling cutlery, and the manageress led them to a table for four, a doctor was touching the eyelids of the man who seemed to be asleep. This 'hospital' was really a first aid room but contained everything needed for emergency, including another doctor; for they had overlapped on their duty rota. The younger doctor saw that the pupils were pin points. He waited for the other, older man, who took one look and said:

"Morphia."

"It looks like it?"

"Self-administered?"

"It could be."

"Do we know how long he's been out?"

"No, we don't."

"The only way to find out would be to question the crew and the passengers," the older man said. He was tired-looking, grey-haired, scraggy.

"If it's that important," remarked the younger man, who went on: "I'll go and find out if the passengers are still at the baggage claim. If they are we can put a temporary hold on them there until the police arrive."

"I'll call the police," the older man volunteered.

He meant, of course, the airport police, who would call the Long Island force if that seemed necessary. The younger man went off. He knew from experience that the best way to check the baggage claim was to see with his own eyes, telephone questions too often received inconclusive and vague answers. This was one of the smaller airport buildings, shared by several airlines, and the baggage was all brought to the conveyors and separated by porters under different flight numbers.

Three people stood by a nearly empty conveyor, above which was an illuminated sign reading: *Flight 212 from Tucson.* A grey-haired porter, red cap set at a rakish angle, came and asked:

"Can I help you, doc?"

"Is this all that's left from Flight 212?"

"Sure is — these three are all that's left."

"Thanks," the doctor said, ruefully.

"There any trouble, doc?"

"There's a sick man," the doctor answered, "If that's trouble."

"It's trouble for someone," the red cap answered, and his wrinkled face and his dark eyes had a tinge of sadness. "You suppose anyone's come to meet the sick person, doc?"

"If they have they may be able to help us," replied the doctor.

But on one had come to meet the man, and after many inquiries and some three hours after the aircraft had landed, a sergeant from the Long Island Homicide Squad and the man in charge of security at the airport, the young doctor and the pilot, met in a room leading off the hospital. Each had a copy of the typewritten report, prepared by the Security Officer after checking with everyone concerned and after going through the passenger's pockets.

It was remarkably comprehensive:

Passenger's name:	Thomas G. Loman
Age:	28
Passport:	U.S.A.
Condition:	Unconscious from morphine poisoning
Period of unconsciousness:	Estimated at one hour after removal from aircraft
Physical condition:	Excellent
Operation or accident scars:	None
Eyes:	Blue
Complexion:	Fair
Hair:	Yellow
Possessions in pockets:	Keys; coins; wallet containing $1,001.1; passport

Travellers cheques:	$5,000
Destination:	London, England
Continuation flight (shown on ticket)	B.O.A.C. 505 22.30 from Kennedy
Baggage in hold: (on ticket)	None
Hand Baggage:	None
Given address in London (on ticket)	c/o Richard Rollison, 25g Gresham Terrace, W.1
Other particulars:	Suspected needle puncture, right forearm. No other punctures.

All the men in the office read this carefully, the Security Officer finishing first. He looked at the others and when the pilot's eyes were raised from the paper, said in a deep voice:

"It sure looks as if the guy was given a shot on the aircraft which put him out."

"But it could have been taken orally," argued the young doctor.

"Or been self-administered," put in the pilot.

"There is no sign of a hypodermic needle in his pockets," stated the Security Officer.

"There might be a disposable hypo in the garbage," contributed the young doctor, eagerly.

"Not in the garbage of Flight 212," replied the Security Officer. "We checked. We can double check, though, we kept the garbage stored, there was good time for that."

"Nice work, Joe," approved the man from Homicide. "What's this about no hand baggage?"

"No hand baggage," stated the Security Officer with assurance he showed in every utterance.

"Did he bring any on board?" inquired the man from Homicide.

This police officer was rather small, plump and pink; he looked less like a New York policeman than anyone present. He was dressed in a well-cut suit and had only one mannerism: raising his right eyebrow from time to time, either speculatively or because he had a twitch. His dark hair was smoothed over his cranium so that streaks of white pate showed through, and the parting was incongruously close to his right ear. Everything about him suggested a man of great personal carefulness; even his hands, the nails of which were manicured although not a particularly good shape.

"He had one small bag," answered the captain.

"Don't they search hand baggage in Tucson?" asked Homicide.

"They search it these days," answered the pilot, "but they don't make out a schedule, Sergeant. If a man's clean of weapons or smuggled goods, he's clean. All these passengers were clean. There was one guy with something in his case which ticked like a bomb but it was his alarm clock, he never trusts hotel clerks to wake him. One guy and a woman had guns, and these were taken away so they had to pick them up at the baggage claim."

"They picked them up," the Security Officer remarked. "From me. They were both in order."

There was a lull in the questions and answers before the pilot asked:

"Did he have baggage checks?"

"Two," agreed the Security Officer.

"So where are his bags?"

"Someone collected them for him."

"Without the claim checks," remarked Homicide.

"You know how it is," said Security wearily. "You pick on one in a dozen to see their check and the one on the baggage they are taking out are the same. We don't have any trouble."

"This," remarked Homicide, heavily, "is trouble. The passenger seems to have been robbed on the aircraft and his baggage taken away from the baggage claim without a claim check. If the guy wants to sue the airline I guess he's got a million dollar case. Joe, what about the passengers on either side of this guy? A passenger on his right could have given him a shot. Or one of the stewardesses. Or — "

"Or anyone passing along the gangway and leaning over for a magazine or, as I told you, it could have been self-administered. We're trying to trace the man who sat on his right but it's not easy — people changed seats a lot, the aircraft wasn't full. The question is, do we ask for details about the guy from Tucson or do we wait until Mr. Thomas G. Loman comes round?"

Now, all eyes were on the man from Homicide, who leaned back in his chair and looked at the young doctor.

"How long will he be under, Doc?"

"There's no way of being sure, it depends on the strength of the shot and the body's reaction to it. Some systems run it out fast, others hold it for a long time. He's been under for more than four hours, now. He might begin to come round at any time."

"Why don't you go and see?" suggested Homicide, in his gentlest voice.

2

Rush!

THE YOUNG MAN with the long face and the spade of a chin was on his back in a room which had three beds, although he was the only occupant. The young doctor went in ahead of the nurse on duty, who said:

"I came in ten minutes ago, doctor, and he hadn't moved."

The doctor stood looking down, and after a few moments, said: "He'll move soon." There were changes in the breathing, in the firmness of the lips and eyes; a kind of relaxation. The doctor touched one of the large, pale eyelids and the young man flinched. The doctor turned round, almost cannoning into the Homicide sergeant, who had come silently on his heels: "Not a case for Homicide," the doctor remarked.

"How soon will he be able to talk?"

"May be half an hour. Morphine patients vary."

"Doc," asked Homicide. "You're sure he's not an addict?"

"I'm sure."

The sergeant nodded, but it was impossible to say whether it was with satisfaction or not. He asked: "Will you let me know when he can talk?" and went out on the doctor's nod of assurance. But he did not immediately go back to the others. He went to the exit

· ·

doors, which opened electronically, and out to his car, parked across the driveway from the taxis. No one else was in it. He slid into the seat and lifted the radio-telephone; soon he was talking to his lieutenant, who had detailed him to this inquiry. He reported lucidly in his gentle voice, and the lieutenant replied:

"So what next?"

"So next we look for a man who jabbed the needle in this guy's arm, a man who could be anywhere in the Metropolitan area of New York, which means one of thirteen million people. And the man we want could have flown out of Kennedy in any one of the three hundred and seven flights which left in the past three hours. If we had a body, we might look. If we have a big heist, we could look. What do you want me to do, Manny?"

"You've got judgment," the lieutenant said. "Why don't you use it."

"That's what I'll do," the sergeant said.

"Luigi," said the lieutenant in a sharper voice: "Are you telling me you've got ideas?"

"Feelings," Sergeant Luigi Tetano retorted.

"You mean a hunch."

"I mean I would like to know more about this Thomas G. Loman and what he's had stolen from him." When he received no answer he went on: "We've been so blinded by hi-jacking we've forgotten the other things that happen. How many passengers from Kennedy complain that their luggage is stolen before they get to the baggage claim?"

"Too many," the lieutenant replied.

"And La Guardia?"

"Too many."

"And sometimes the passengers who lose their bags are called to the telephone on phoney messages and some-times they go into the rest rooms and sometimes they make a telephone call and sometimes they're met by their families and the reunion takes a lot of time. So when they reach the baggage claim, no baggage."

"Right," the lieutenant confirmed.

"It's wrong," said Luigi Tetano. "This time they dope the guy so they can take his hand baggage as well."

"Luigi," the lieutenant observed, "it doesn't have to be the same gang. Okay, there is a gang operating and okay, we haven't found it, but this could be different. It *is* different in one way, because of the fact the guy was doped. So it could be a different job altogether, different people — oh, come on you know what I mean."

"Sure," said Luigi. "It could also be the same mob going a step further."

"So it could be."

"Do I get to follow my nose?" asked Luigi.

"Sure."

"Wherever it takes me?"

"Sure," the lieutenant answered.

"That's fine," breathed Luigi. "That's very good, Manny. I'll call you again."

He replaced the receiver and switched off, then sat back with his eyes half-closed. This made him look a little younger: baby-faced. Overhead a four-engined aircraft roared, others seemed to be landing and taking off every minute. Taxis were arriving, picking up passengers, going off into the complex of roads which served the mammoth airport. Dusk was falling, and lights were beginning to show in the sky and on the ground. He opened his eyes wide and looked at his watch: it was seven-fifteen. He got out of the car and went back to the room where the others were sitting, and as he opened the door the Security Officer was saying:

"Should I go look for him?"

"I want to go home," complained the pilot. "I've got a date."

They looked round as he entered — including the young doctor, who was sitting against a table, hands at the side. Sergeant Luigi Tetano ignored the others and looked at him.

"He come round, Doc?"

"Yes."

"I'll come and see him." Luigi looked round at the others and went on in the same flat voice: "If anyone wants home, okay. But maybe I'll have to call him back. And maybe we'll need to see all members of the crew of that flight. In half an hour I should know. Can your date wait for half an hour?" He looked at the pilot.

"My wife is a patient woman," answered the pilot.

Luigi and the young doctor went across the crowded terminal building to the hospital, and heard the nurse in the private room, talking; protesting. When the two men entered, the long-faced young passenger was on his feet, and he proved to be very tall and lean. He was standing on one leg, pulling his trousers on, pyjamas were loose on the floor. The nurse was saying:

"You're crazy to behave like this. You ought to rest."

"Yes, ma'am," the young man drawled. "I always was kind of crazy." But he dropped on to the side of the bed, obviously with weariness, and there was a worried expression on his face: "I sure could drink some coffee."

"If you will stop acting like a big boy — "

"Could you use some coffee?" the doctor asked Luigi.

"Sure could."

"Honey, why don't you go and get us some coffee from the restaurant," suggested the young doctor. "They could send it over with a boy." He opened the door for her and she went out, while the tall young man sat on the edge of the bed. He had on a brown and yellow checked shirt, open at the neck, and well-tailored, sand-coloured slacks. His legs and arms were more muscular than one might have expected, and he had surprisingly broad and powerful-looking shoulders. He gave a slow, lazy smile, showing teeth both big and white.

"Thanks," he said. "Will one of you tell me what happened?"

"You were drugged with morphia," Luigi told him.

"You were unconscious with morphine poisoning." The doctor was more precise.

"Your hand baggage and your checked baggage was stolen," the Homicide man stated, "but no one took your money or your travellers' cheques."

The young man named Thomas G. Loman put a hand to his forehead; that might have been to hide his expression of bewilderment. And no wonder, thought the Homicide man, the fellow had plenty to be bewildered about. Apart from the movement of his arm and hand, he kept very still. He seemed to be like that for a long time, before he asked in a muffled voice:

"Do you have the time?"

"Twenty of eight," answered Luigi. "Still night-time!"

"I have to be on a flight to London, England, at ten-thirty."

"You have to check in at nine-thirty," said Luigi. "You have plenty of time."

"You need to rest," the doctor said.

"I can rest on the flight, I guess."

"What about your baggage?" Luigi asked.

"So I've no baggage." At last Thomas G. Loman lowered his hand — and on the same instant the door opened and the nurse came in with a tray. "I've lost baggage before."

"You mean you've had some stolen before?" Luigi demanded.

The young man looked at him levelly, and slowly shook his head. The nurse put the tray down on a bedside table and began to pour coffee. She had some cookies on a plate, also.

"I said lost," repeated Loman.

"I said stolen."

"Can you prove it was stolen?"

"I can prove you had a shot in the arm. Look hard enough and you will see the puncture."

The young man said: "So I put myself to sleep."

"With what?"

"A shot," Loman answered.

"Where did you put the hypo?"

"Down the pan," Loman answered. "I went along there and gave myself a shot and put the plastic hypo down the pan and came back to my seat."

The nurse managed to ask: "Do you use cream in your coffee?"

"Sure," said Loman.

"Not for me," answered the doctor.

"I use facts," Luigi said. "Why did you dope yourself, Loman?"

"Like the doctor said, I need sleep."

"Like I said, I need facts," retorted Luigi. He picked up a cup of coffee which had neither cream nor sugar, and sipped; his gaze did not once leave Loman's face, but the young man stared back without apparent embarrassment.

"What did you have in your baggage?" Luigi asked.

"Clothes."

"In your hand baggage?"

"A razor and toiletries and two books."

"What kind of books?"

"Adult books," the young man answered amiably. "I'm an adult." He finished his coffee, and turned to the doctor as if he were no longer interested in the policeman. The nurse had moved away and was looking from one to the other as if she could make nothing of the conversation or of the situation. "Doctor," went on Loman, "I'm appreciative of the trouble you've taken and I'll be glad to pay your fee right now. That's if someone will hand me my billfold," he added with a boyish grin.

"The nurse will get that," the doctor replied. "You take it easy."

"As soon as I'm dressed and in the B.O.A.C. lounge I'll take it easy," Loman assured him. "I don't need to eat, there will be food on the aircraft." He finished the coffee, and smiled at the nurse. "Okay for me to have the rest of my clothes now?"

She answered: "I still think you're crazy."

"My folks often used to say just the same thing," Loman assured her, but now there was something so attractive in his smile that she half-laughed, and fetched his jacket.

Luigi went outside, and found the Security Officer hovering. The man crossed to him at once, and asked in his hard, controlled voice:

"Is he making a complaint?"

"He will, if he's no fool."

"Luigi," the Security Officer said, "you don't have to be like this."

"It's just the way I am," replied Luigi, and went on: "He's going to fly on to London. He'll ask you to look for his luggage and send it on to him, and if I were you that's exactly what I would do."

The Security Officer said: "So there's no complaint." He looked relieved as he nodded and moved away, almost as Thomas G. Loman came out. He pretended not to notice the man from Homicide but went with long strides towards the air line's desk and made his complaint about lost luggage, asking for it to be sent on. A young girl with a magnificent honey-brown skin took details, then asked:

"What is your forwarding address in London, sir?"

"Care of Richard Rollison," Loman answered. "Number 25g, Gresham Terrace, London, W.1." He spelled out both the name of the man and the street, then moved away. He did not bump into Luigi, only because Luigi darted back quickly. Loman towered a head and shoulders above the policeman, who asked:

"You want to go to the B.O.A.C. terminal?"

"I don't want to go to police headquarters."

"Something on your conscience?" flashed Luigi.

"I've got a flight waiting for me."

"Loman," Luigi said. "I won't give you the runaround. I'll take you to B.O.A.C. departures if that's where you want to go."

"That's where I want to go," the man from Tucson declared.

Luigi Tetano drove him there with the speed and roadway knowledge more characteristic of a taxi driver than a policeman, and watched him check in. No one appeared to be surprised that he was early, the only surprise was about his lack of luggage. Soon, he went up the escalator and out of Luigi's sight. The policeman left his car again and went to a telephone booth just inside the departure building, while aircraft roared and screeched overhead. He dialled a friend on the staff of the *New York Times*, and when the other man answered, said:

"Ben, you know London pretty well, don't you?"

"I'm not sure I don't know it better than New York," answered Ben. "Are you forgetting I was the London correspondent for five years?"

"I half-remembered," Luigi replied drily. "Can you tell me anything about a guy named Rollison?"

Without even an instant's pause the other repeated, like an echo: "*Rollison!* Richard Rollison?"

"That's right, he lives — "

"Luigi," the newspaperman said, "I know plenty about Rollison. If you take my advice, you won't tangle with him."

"I don't believe the criminal I won't tangle with exists," retorted Luigi. "What's so special about him?"

"He's not a crook," answered the *Times* man. " 'Private eye' isn't the right description but you would call him one. *He* doesn't know the criminal he won't tangle with, either. He — " there was a pause, a sharp intake of breath, another pause, then a deep-voiced question redolent of suspicion. "What do you want with the Toff?"

"The who?"

"The Toff. T — O — F — F," the *Times* man spelled out. He allowed just enough time for the spelling to register on Luigi's mind before repeating: "I'll tell you what I know about the Toff when I know why you want the information. You come clean, Luigi, and I will."

"Off the record," Luigi said.

"Off the record," agreed the newspaperman. "In the beginning, anyway."

"Okay," agreed Luigi. He told the story in outline, answered a few questions, and then in a tone of deep finality he declared: "That's plenty, Ben. Now you tell me all you know about this Rollison — this Toff. What *is* a Toff, anyway?"

3

A Toff is a Toff

THE HONOURABLE RICHARD ROLLISON, known to so
many as the Toff, stood at a corner of his large, flat-
topped, heirloom desk on the top floor of 25g Gresham
Terrace, London, W.1, the telephone held in one hand
and a pencil in the other. Silence was coming from the
telephone, the faintest of aromas creeping from the
domestic quarters of this unusual, indeed unique flat,
as Rollison gazed pensively at his Trophy Wall.

He was a tall man, and lean.

Like Thomas G. Loman, he was surprisingly strong
and muscular.

Unlike Thomas G. Loman, he was remarkably handsome, classic in the Ronald Colman style, with the same
hint of virility and humanity in his good looks. The years
had passed lightly over him despite many dangers and
crises, his hair was dark with only a touch of grey here
and there, adding a note of distinction. He had well-
marked eyebrows and his skin had a weathered look;
what few lines there were at forehead and eyes seemed
due more to concentration than to years.

He was not young in the sense that teenagers are
considered to be young, but he was a century away
from being old. In most moods, and this was one, he

had exemplary patience, and the silence from the telephone did not worry him.

In fact, he was day-dreaming.

It was comparatively early in the morning; half-past eight. He had been at the home of friends the night before, and back here late, so when the telephone had disturbed him he had not woken easily. It had been the overseas operator to ask if he could take a call from New York in half an hour's time. So he had had time for his tea in bed, to scan the newspapers, even to shave. By the time the telephone bell had rung again he had been in this room. Waiting.

And studying the Trophies.

That was his man's word for the strange assortment of objects on the wall behind the desk, and it was a good choice, for each was indeed a trophy of the hunt. In every case the quarry had been human, in most cases a man, but some had been women.

All were murderers.

Many had been hanged, before the laws of England had so changed that men and women were no longer hanged by the neck until they were dead, but sentenced, on conviction of murder, to 'life' imprisonment. Rollison kept an open mind on the subject of capital punishment but did not think that 'life' should prove, as it so often did, no more than nine or ten years in prison. Yet there were murderers whom he would have let off scot-free had he been judge and jury.

But none such as those he had been hunting until they had died or had been caught and tried, and later represented on this wall. For these trophies were of deadly killers; mostly evil men. The small tube of poisons reminded him of the hideous doctor who gave prostitutes a drug to make them scream and writhe — and while they were in contortions of agony the doctor possessed

them. The top hat had two bullet holes; the second had
knocked the hat off his head, some nine years ago. The
lipstick had contained potassium cyanide, so that the user,
breaking a thin coating protecting the lethal dose, had
daubed her lips and died. Even the nylon stocking, looking solitary and strangely seductive draped over a skeletal
foot, had been used to strangle a woman.

These things Rollison remembered as he waited.

He saw his man, Jolly, appear at the door leading from
the kitchen, and sadly shook his head; Jolly by now,
would have bacon and eggs all ready for the pan and
would be exasperated by this delay.

Suddenly, a man said: "Mr. Rollison?" in an unmistakable American voice.

"Yes," Rollison said, almost startled.

"Mr. Rollison, I'm sorry to bother you at this time,
but my name is Selly, Jim Selly, of the *New York Times*.
You might even remember me."

Vaguely he did, thought Rollison, but he made a
non-committal noise, and allowed Selly to go on:

"Mr. Rollison, are you expecting a visit from a friend
from Arizona?"

"From where?" asked Rollison, startled again.

"From Tucson, Arizona."

"I'm afraid I have to say that I'm not," replied
Rollison. "I'm not expecting a visitor from anywhere in
America, and I don't think I know anyone in Tucson —
or Arizona, for that matter." He wondered why a newspaperman should call to ask such a question, but newspapermen were strange creatures with insatiable appetites
for new twists and angles, so he did not wonder deeply.
"Why do you want to know?"

"Are you *sure* you don't know anyone from Tucson,
Arizona?" Selly sounded acutely disappointed.

"I am positive," insisted Rollison.

"This man's name is Loman — L-O-M-A-N. Is *he* a friend of yours?"

"Not," answered Rollison, feeling wide awake for the first time, "unless he has changed his name. Why do you think I know a Mr. Loman?"

"He said that he knew you," Selly answered.

"Oh," said Rollison, baffled. "And is he on the way to see me, do you say?"

"Yes," replied the newspaperman, and he paused. Rollison had a feeling that he was going to ask again 'You're sure you don't know the man' but thought better of it. "Well, thank you," Selly went on. "Goodbye, sir."

He rang off.

Rollison put down his receiver, still puzzled and more than a little frustrated. Selly might at least have told him more about this Loman from Arizona. He was contemplating the wall without really seeing it when Jolly appeared again. Jolly was half a head shorter than Rollison, an elderly man who had sad-looking, dark brown eyes, deep lines all over his face and a dewlap which had become wizened; he had the general appearance of a man who had once been fat but, after much self-sacrifice, had become thin; and dyspeptic. He had served Rollison since his schooldays, and these men were close friends.

Jolly was dressed in striped trousers and a white shirt and wore a green baize apron.

"Shall I put the eggs on, sir?"

"Jolly," said Rollison, "do we know a man named Loman?"

After a moment's reflection, Jolly answered: "No, sir. Should we?"

"I suspect that we are going to find out. Yes, put on the eggs, and I'll tell you about the call while I have breakfast. Have you had yours?"

"Oh, yes, sir."

"Then have some coffee while I eat," said Rollison.

Between now and breakfast being served there would be no time to dress, so he went to a wall which was at angles with the trophy one and took down a World Gazetteer, then thumbed the pages until he found Tucson, pronounced, it was said, Teu-*sonn*. It was a city of some three hundred and fifty thousand people, with mountains to the north and south, the east and west. There the sun shone on most days of the year and it could become much too hot but seldom too cold. Near it were many mines, mostly producing copper, and the final word was: 'Tucson is one of the five quickest growing cities in the United States judged on population.'

"Humm," Rollison said to himself.

Immediately, Jolly appeared with a tray which he placed on a table in a small, raised dining-alcove at one end of this large room. Rollison set to, Jolly drank coffee, Rollison told the story briefly, and Jolly remarked:

"I remember Mr. Selly, sir."

"You do?" Rollison was intrigued.

"He came one day when you were out," Jolly informed him, "and asked me what a Toff was."

"Oh," said Rollison, still further intrigued. "What did you tell him?"

"That a toff is a toff, sir."

"I am sure that conveyed everything he needed to know," Rollison said drily.

"Of course I elaborated somewhat," went on Jolly urbanely, "but basically it *is* a difficult term to define, especially to this generation." When Rollison speared a piece of bacon, obviously expecting him to go on, Jolly continued: "I told him that a toff was a gentleman of high social standing who exerted himself to do great good among the less fortunate members of society."

"Oh," Rollison said. "Can't we do better than that?"

"Can *you*, sir?" inquired Jolly.

"I shall think about it," Rollison decided, and after a liberal helping of bacon and eggs, spread butter and a dark-coloured marmalade on toast, finished breakfast and went to his room to dress. It was not one of his good mornings, for his attempt to define a 'toff' proved both disconcerting and abortive. He found that Jolly had made his bed and laid out a medium weight suit of heather colour, perhaps as satisfactory as any for this autumn day. "A toff," he said in a complaining voice, "is a man who gets waited on hand and foot and is rich enough to give hand-outs." He knew that was not fair to himself, laughed aloud, dressed, and was going into the big room when the telephone bell rang again.

"I'll get it!" he called, and this time sat down with his back to the Trophy Wall, plucked up the receiver, and said: "Richard Rollison."

"Good morning, Rolly," said a man with a familiar voice. "And what have you been up to?"

"*Bill!*" Rollison almost groaned.

"That's right. Come on, now. You might as well confess."

"Bill," interrupted Rollison in a tone of mock desperation. "You are the very man I need. Who better than Chief Detective Superintendent William Grice of New Scotland Yard to tell me what I am? Bill — can you define 'a Toff?"

There was silence.

He had at least gained time to think, but thinking did not take him far. Grice was both old adversary and old friend, and had been concerned in most of the cases remembered on the Trophy Wall. Frequently, when he, Rollison, became involved in an inquiry it was before the police discovered that there was anything to inquire about. At such times Grice was likely to call and ask: "What have you been up to?" Rollison could not think of a single recent activity which could justify the question.

At last, Grice said: "A toff is a toff, of course."

"You're a great help," said Rollison heavily. "Nothing."

"What?"

"I have been up to nothing which might interest you."

"That is the one thing about you I would never believe," retorted Grice. "You can't expect me to believe it, either."

"Bill," Rollison said, pleadingly, "be more specific, will you? It has been one of those mornings. I can't get any sense out of anybody and least of all from myself. What makes you think I have been 'up to something'?"

Again there was a pause, doubtless while Grice decided whether he was stalling or whether he was genuinely baffled. Rollison made himself more comfortable in his chair. Suddenly, Grice said: "Just a minute, Rolly," and Rollison held on, hearing voices in the background; someone had come in Grice's office. This time Rollison felt the stirring of impatience; he seemed to have done nothing but hold on at the telephone all the morning. The delay was very short, and Grice came back in a stronger voice: "What do you know of a man named Thomas G. or C. Loman?"

Rollison sat bolt upright in his chair.

"And don't say 'nothing'," Grice almost barked.

"Bill," said Rollison, faintly, "I know next to nothing. An American newspaperman named Selly called from New York this morning and asked me if I were expecting a visit from a man named Loman. I answered truly: I was not. He then wanted to know if I knew any Loman.

I answered as truly: I did not. He added that Loman
hails from the city of Tucson, in — "

"I know where he hails from," interrupted Grice. "Is
this gospel, Rolly? You really don't know him?"

"Until this morning I had never heard of him. I
couldn't have placed Tucson with any accuracy on a
map, either."

"Never mind Tucson." There was another pause and
a murmur of voices, as if Grice were in consultation in
his office. Then Grice came back and demanded in one
breath: "If you don't know him, how is it he has your
name and address as his final destination in London on
his travel documents."

"He *has*?" exclaimed Rollison.

"I have his ticket in front of me, and on it your
address is quoted as his English destination."

"You know," Rollison said. "I wish he would come. I
would like to ask him a thing or two."

"Well," Grice said, "he can't."

The phrase struck an ominous note and moved
Rollinson's emotions from bewilderment with an under-
tone of frustration to apprehension. He did not ask why
Thomas G. Loman could not come to see him, but
knew of at least one very good reason: that he was dead.

Grice went on slowly, as if grudgingly: "Not yet, at all
events."

The devil, thought Rollison, he's having me on.
Aloud, he asked: "Is he hurt?"

"He's unconscious."

"What put him out?" demanded Rollison, sharply.

"A shot of morphia," Grice stated, without any hesitation at all. "When the aircraft arrived at Heath Row
this morning he was found unconscious in his seat. At
first the stewardesses thought he was asleep, but it is
much more than that. He's in the airport hospital now,

and I've just had the report saying that he's under morphine and that there are hypodermic needle punctures in his right and left forearms." There was a long pause which could only be called pregnant, before Grice demanded in a voice laden with doubt: "Are you sure you don't know him? Are you sure you're not up to something you've forgotten to tell us about?"

Very slowly, Rollison answered: "I am quite sure, William."

"Then why the devil should he have been coming to see you?" demanded Grice. "He's got no luggage and no money in his wallet. His American passport is valid. Either he left New York quite empty handed or else he's been robbed."

4

Face to Face

"BILL," ROLLISON SAID with quiet persistence, after a long, pregnant-type pause, "I can't answer any of the questions about this man because I don't know a thing about him. Unless — "

"*Ah!*" broke in Grice, semi-triumphant.

"Unless he's using a false name, which would presumably mean using a false passport," Rollison finished.

"I have known friends of yours do such things," Grice observed, cuttingly.

"Bill," said Rollison in his gentlest voice. "You aren't exactly in the friendliest of moods this morning, are you?"

There was a short pause, followed by a staccato exclamation, before Grice said in tacit agreement:

"I must have got out of bed the wrong side. Can you go to the airport?"

"To identify the man, if by chance I do know him under some other name?"

"Yes."

Rollison pondered. He had a committee meeting for a fund-raising group for Cancer Research but they could get on without him, and he had a luncheon appointment with his accountant, who could easily be put off; and in any case a 'no' would probably make Grice's mood even more difficult. So he said in the most conciliatory tone:

"Yes, Bill, I can leave here in twenty minutes or so. Will you be there?"

"I wish I could be but I've a Commissioner's meeting," Grice answered. The overhanging threat of that could partly explain his mood. "You know Paterson of the Airport Police, don't you?"

"Slightly."

"I'll tell him to expect you," Grice promised. "And thanks."

"I really can't wait to meet Thomas G. or C. Loman," Rollison told him.

"I've just made sure it's G., as in George," asserted Grice.

"Thanks. I'll let you know how I get on," Rollison promised, and rang off.

For a few moments he sat back, frowning at the ceiling, and did not look round when Jolly came in. Jolly would have heard the conversation on the kitchen extension: it was accepted that he should listen to all but personal calls, thus saving the need for explanation on matters he would need to know about in any case. "What do you make of it?" Rollison asked.

"Peculiar is one word, sir." Jolly came further into the room.

"Suspicious?" asked Rollison.

"In the sense that this could be an attempt to involve you in some affair without you knowing?" asked Jolly.

"Yes."

"Conceivably so," Jolly admitted. "Yes indeed, sir, that *is* possible."

Rollison pushed back his chair, stood up, and jingled coins and some keys in his pocket. He studied Jolly in a preoccupied way, and the flat was silent as the two men were still. The shadow of the Trophy Wall seemed to loom about them until Rollison threw the shadow off and said lightly:

"Telephone apologies for my two appointments, will you?"

"I will indeed, sir."

"If I'm not going to be in for lunch, I'll telephone you." Jolly would be athirst for news, and it would be stark cruelty simply to stay away if the affair of Thomas G. Loman promised any interesting developments. "I'll get going," he added. "I'll take the Bristol."

"Very good, sir," Jolly said.

Rollison went to his room, checked his change, keys and wallet, then went back to the big room. He could not say what moved him to go to the window, a point of vantage in times of excitement. By standing to one side he could see most of the street — in fact all of it in each direction except the few square yards immediately in front of this house. Times out of number he had come here and noticed someone watching his flat.

More than once, such a precaution had saved his life.

Now, he saw a girl, watching: she was actually looking upwards.

Taken by surprise, he studied her as closely as he could from this distance, and in the foreshortened perspective. She was attractive, with glossy brown hair which fell to her shoulders. She wore a bell-bottom pant-suit in olive green, itself most attractive. Had he noticed her walking along the street he would have thought simply: nice. She looked up and down the street and then up at the window again; had he moved a foot closer, she would have seen him.

He called: "Jolly!"

Jolly was in the room in a trice.

"Have you ever seen this girl before?" asked Rollison,

making way for his man. "The one in the olive green trouser-suit."

Jolly, who had to go closer to the window in order to see out, said simply: "No, sir."

"But we'll recognise her if we see her again, won't we?" Rollison mused.

"Would you like me to follow you in the Austin, sir?" asked Jolly, no doubt hopefully.

"So that you can follow her if she follows me," inferred Rollison. "No, I don't think so. I'd rather you were here in case some quick action on the home front is called for. But watch to see if she follows me out of the street."

"I certainly will," promised Jolly.

Rollison went towards the front door.

The unique quality of the apartment was that it had a lounge hall with a passage leading towards the domestic quarters and the bedrooms, and a door into the big study-cum-living room with its dining alcove. Along a continuation of this was a passage also leading to bedrooms and the domestic quarters. Two people could play hide-and-seek for a long time in the flat. Rollison, encouraged and at times inspired by Jolly, had made some refinements. Both doors — the front one and the one leading to the fire escape from the kitchen — could be locked and made virtually impregnable. So could all the windows. Moreover, above the lintel of the front door was an ingenious contraption based on the principle of the periscope. By glancing up from inside, one could see the landing and the staircase beyond; and so be forewarned if anyone lurked there.

No one did.

He opened the door and went down three flights of stairs, each flight divided with a half-landing. The stairs were of stone but covered now with druggeting of a dark purple colour. He ran down them, humming to himself, opened the street door and stepped out, blithely, and slammed the door behind him.

The girl was on the other side of the road.

Rollison showed no apparent interest in her, but turned right, towards other streets and, round the corner, a mews where he kept his car and Jolly's. His was a two-year-old, grey-coloured Bristol, a hand-manufactured car which gave him much sensuous pleasure. He noticed an open M.G. sports car close to the entrance of the mews before unlocking his garage.

The M.G. was not empty when he drove out; the brown-haired girl was at the wheel and vibration of the exhaust pipe with its stainless steel fan-tail told him the engine was turning. He drove along Gresham Terrace, a street of tall, three-storey houses, some drab, some newly painted, and the girl followed. He crossed a stream of traffic in Piccadilly, to turn right; and so did she. He took the underpass at Hyde Park corner but she did not; yet in Knightsbridge, opposite Harrods, she was close behind.

Occasionally, she appeared to lose him but as he drove on to the short section of the M4 Motorway, there she was; and when he went down to the cavern-like turn on to the Great West Road, she was on his heels. Until then he had simply allowed her to follow, but suddenly he put on speed, turned left at the first traffic lights into a road with houses on one side and the playing fields of what seemed a private school on the other. He took the first turn right along here, and swung behind some trees; this was a place where he had caught followers before.

She passed the end of the street he was in, turning her head to try to see the Bristol. He was close enough to see the distress on her face; a kind of fear. There were

no turnings off the street she was driving down and some
distance along it was a level crossing; she might go on,
hoping to catch up. Or she might turn back, thinking he
had turned into the driveway of a house. He pulled out
as soon as she had disappeared, and followed her — put
on a burst of speed and suddenly brought the Bristol
alongside the M.G.

"Pull in," he ordered, and when she hesitated he
roared: "Now!" and steered towards the smaller car.
She pulled in quickly but did not jolt the car; nor did
she stall the engine. He drew so close that the cars were
almost touching before he went on: "Now, what is it all
about?"

She would probably lie.

He noticed one man farther along the street, and two
women at different windows, watching; each had no
doubt noticed the way he had forced the girl into the
kerb.

She stared at him, and he at her, each framed in an
open car window. She had the most beautiful golden
brown eyes, something he hadn't been able to see from
the flat window, and a superb complexion. He thought
he read fear in her eyes, and began to wonder how best
to ease that fear at least enough to make her talk, when
she said:

"I can't believe it."

She had a pleasant voice, English as a summer
meadow.

"What can't you believe?" he asked, trying not to be
too accusing.

"You are even *more* handsome than they told me,"
she declared.

He stared. She smiled, tremulously. He snorted, and
then, unable to help himself, began to utter a deep

throated chuckle; immediately relief showed in her eyes, and she relaxed too.

"You *are* more handsome," she asserted.

"I can't tell you how proud I am," Rollison said, and chuckled again. "You are much prettier than you looked from my flat window."

"You *saw* me?"

"You intended me to see you," he stated flatly.

Earnestly, and putting a hand towards him as if to touch his face, she said in that sweet-sounding voice:

"It's impossible — I can't even *hope* to deceive you?" Her eyes were huge.

"It would be fascinating to find out what would happen if you tried," he remarked. "With most men no doubt you find it easy. Are you busy?"

"Well, not just now."

"What do you mean, not just now?"

"I *was* busy, because I wanted to talk to you," she told him, "and simply didn't know how to go about it. It's as pleasant as it's easy."

"*I'm* busy," he interrupted. "I've an urgent job to do."

Her face fell. "Oh," she said, as if crestfallen.

"But we could talk on the way," he added.

"On the way where?"

"Where I am going. You could come in my car and talk to me while I drive, a process called killing two birds with one stone."

She gave a funny little shudder, as if not liking what he had said about killing. If possible, her eyes grew even rounder and more huge.

"Are you serious?" she demanded.

"Very serious."

"Very well," the girl decided, "I'll come. Will you remember where I've left my car?"

"Yes," he assured her. "This is where I always have

the people who follow me park; that's how I was able to shake you off so easily."

"Oh," she said, looking at him dubiously. Then she added earnestly: "I believe you're pulling my leg."

"Never!" he breathed.

She got out of her car on the pavement side, pulled the leather apron over the seats, against possible rain, then came round to him, clutching a large handbag made of two-tone canvas matching her suit perfectly. He had half expected her to run away but she showed no sign of that at all. He eased the Bristol away from her car, leaned across to open the far door for her. She got in with easy grace, studying his profile.

"Side face, too?" he inquired.

"In every way," she assured him.

"Before long I shall feel flattered. Do you mind opening your handbag?"

"Doing *what*?" she gasped.

"Opening your handbag," he repeated, pleasantly. "I just want to make as sure as I can that you're not carrying a gun." He beamed. "Please."

She opened the handbag as wide as it would go. Inside was the expected variety of toiletries and make-up articles, a small purse, a thin wad of one pound notes, some keys — and a centre pocket which was fastened by a zip. He touched this with his forefinger, and she opened it.

Inside was a small, pearl-handled automatic.

"Ah," he breathed.

"I live alone," she answered. "And I often travel alone."

"And that pistol keeps you safe and so fills you with confidence, no doubt," he said. "May I see it?" He took it out of the pocket of the bag and it fitted snugly on the palm of his hand, one of the smallest and most attractive-looking lethal weapons he had ever seen. "Do you have a licence?"

"Yes."

He pulled the holder away and took out the clip; there were six bullets, each one of which would kill. He replaced the clip and placed the pistol back in the bag, zipping it up smoothly. "Thank you. What's your name?"

"Pamela Brown," she answered.

He stifled the impulse to echo 'Brown' with obvious disbelief, then gave her the bag and started the engine. He turned in a private carriageway, still watched by the two women but no longer by the man; a dog came racing up to the car, barking wildly, until at last Rollison was heading back towards the Great West Road. Not until he was on it, putting on speed, did he ask:

"Why do you want to talk to me?"

"Because I believe you can help," she answered.

"In what way do you need help?" asked Rollison. "You seem to be able to take very good care of yourself."

"In some ways I can," agreed the girl who called herself Pamela Brown, "but in others a woman is so helpless. You see," she went on with the ingenuousness which characterised her, even though it could be more assumed than natural. "I'm not a supporter of the Women's Liberation Movement, I don't think men and women are equal. Some jobs men do superbly well and women make a mess of. Don't you agree?"

"It works the other way round, too," said Rollison modestly.

"Oh, yes," she said, "I couldn't agree more." She waited until he passed two big trucks which were going

too fast, then as he approached the roundabout where
the road divided, one heading south west and the other
due west — and past the entrance to the airport. "The
real truth is I wanted to talk to you about Tom Loman.
That is who you're going to meet, isn't it? Tom Loman,
at London airport?"

5

Motor-Cyclist

THERE WAS NO POINT in lying.

Even had he been tempted to, Rollison doubted whether a lie would fool this girl, for his start of surprise had actually made him swing the wheel a fraction, enough to scare a driver who was passing at furious speed on the inside. This man wrenched his wheel and pressed his horn in a long and desperate wail. Rollison straightened out, watched only the road ahead, and said:

"I don't know."

"Really, Mr. Rollison!"

"I don't know," repeated Rollison. "I am going to see a man at London airport who is said to be a Thomas G. Loman, but whether he is or not I can't possibly say."

After a few moments of silence, the girl responded: "I don't understand you at all."

"I've never seen and before this morning never heard of any Thomas G. Loman. So whether the man I'm going to see is Thomas G. Loman I can't say." When she didn't reply to that immediately he asked: "Don't you understand that, either?"

"Oh, yes," she said. "I understand. I'm in the same boat."

"Fascinating," retorted Rollison. "How?"

The traffic lights at the turn off into the airport were

looming up, and he was already in the right lane. In the distance great jet engines were roaring, in the sky half a dozen aircraft flew at different levels, while one monster took off, dark fumes streaming from its jets and fading slowly into the contaminated air.

"I represent the other claimants," she stated at last.

"Claimants to what?" asked Rollison, turning left on a green light.

"Goodness!" Pamela Brown exclaimed. "You really don't know, do you?"

She sounded amazed. He was aware that she was staring at him and could imagine how huge her starry eyes had become, could imagine that her lips were parted so that her teeth glinted. He was sure that this pose was as artificial as much else about her, although she might have practised for so long that it seemed natural to her. He veered towards the nearside of the road, looking for a place to pull in — how was it one could be so familiar with a roadway and yet know so little about it?

There was no pull off; he would have to drive on, under the tunnel which led to the airport proper, and find a spot there. He looked in his mirror to make sure he could pull out again, and saw a motor-cyclist, not far behind catching up slowly. The rider wore a tall white crash helmet and goggles, a leather jacket and leggings; and he was small on a mini-machine.

He was guiding the motor-cycle with one hand.

He was looking at the Bristol, not beyond it and along the road.

Quite suddenly, Rollison shot out his left arm and flung it round Pamela Brown's shoulders, thrust her down beneath the level of the window, and bent as low over the steering wheel as he dared. The roar of the motor-cycle suddenly became deafening. He twisted his head round so that he could see the driving mirror, and managed to jam on the brakes. The car jolted to a stand-still, the motor-cycle roared past, the car struck the concrete road verge, bumped on to the grass, and shuddered.

Rollison heard cars passing, followed suddenly by a sharp explosion, like the back-fire of a car.

But it wasn't a back-fire.

Fragments of metal struck the windscreen, the sides of the car and the bonnet, clods of earth and turf smacked on to the metal and into the road. As they did so, Rollison peered ahead. Through a gap between two pieces of soil, saw the motor-cyclist disappearing at the roundabout. He heard brakes squealing and a car horn wailing, and heard Pamela Brown ask in a strangled voice:

"What — what was that?"

At the same moment a young man put his head through the window, and asked tensely:

"Are you all right?"

"Yes," Rollison said, straightening up and letting Pamela go. "Thanks to the grace of God, and — "

"Thanks to your speed of action," contradicted the young man, who had dark, wavy and attractive hair and a pleasant face. "I've never seen anyone jam on brakes so fast. Did you know what he was going to do?"

"I had an idea he was up to no good when I saw the way he was behaving," Rollison replied. "Were you behind?"

"Fifty yards or so, yes. I saw *every*thing. The motor-cyclist put on a fantastic burst of speed and tossed something into the car — well, *at* the car. The way you stopped made him miss." He withdrew his head from the car as if to peer over the top, and said in a voice which sounded farther away: "My God, look at that hole!" He bobbed down again. "You know," he went on in a bewildered voice. "I think he meant to kill you."

"It looks very much like that to me, too," Rollison conceded gravely, and he smiled up into the young man's eyes. "Do you know the airport well?"

"Pretty well," answered the other. "I'm on building maintenance here."

"Can you go to the Airport Police and tell them what happened and give them this?" Rollison handed the other a visiting card which simply gave his name and address. "Ask for Chief Inspector Paterson, he's expecting me."

The young man glanced at the card, and then stared back at Rollison in stupefaction:

"You — you're the *Toff*?"

"Some call me that," Rollison agreed.

"Good Lord!" The young man still looked dumb-struck, but he wasn't and before Rollison could urge him to hurry, he said: "*Now* I know how you came to act so quickly. You're as good as your reputation. Yes, stay here, I'll go and get the Inspector."

He turned and ran back to his car. A moment later he passed them in a green mini Morris, going like a streak of lightning. No one else had stopped, but dozens of drivers had passed the be-spattered car and the hole in the ground and the smoke still rising from it.

Throughout all this, Pamela Brown had sat very still. Rollison did not even know whether she had looked at the young man, or at the hole, or whether she was dazed from shock. Now, he turned towards her, and as he did so she shifted round in her seat, placed her hands on his cheeks and drew his head towards her, then quite deliberately kissed him on the lips. When she drew back, she said:

"I shall never be able to thank you."

"Just do that regularly and you'd be surprised," Rollison retorted.

"*Please* don't make light of it," she pleaded, and tears were close to her eyes. "You saved my life."

"If I did, I also saved mine."

"I would never have believed anyone could have acted so quickly. It wasn't until Baby Blue Eyes explained that I realised what had happened. The motor-cyclist actually threw a bomb."

"Which makes him a bad man."

"And if it had come into the car — "

"It didn't," Rollison interrupted. "Pamela Brown, we've no time to brood on might have beens. He certainly meant to kill the pair of us and whether he was after one or the other or both we'll soon find out. Do you know why anyone should want to kill me?"

In a subdued voice, Pamela answered: "No."

"That makes two of us. Do you want to be interviewed by the Airport Police and then by the men from the Yard?"

Slowly, she shook her head.

"Not really," she said.

"Then now is your only chance to avoid it," Rollison told her. "If you take all the short cuts you'll see — "

"Oh, I know where the taxis are," she interrupted. "You'll really let me go?"

"I shall expect dinner tonight, tête à tête, at my flat."

Her eyes lit up.

"That would be lovely!"

"Don't get yourself killed before then," he warned. "And be careful crossing the road."

She was already sliding along the seat towards the far door, looking at him but groping for the handle. She found it and opened the door, turned to get out, then stopped on the edge of the seat, turning her head as she cried:

"What's the name of the street where my car is parked?"

"Hood Lane," he replied without hesitation.

"Thank you," she said, got out, bent down to stare at him intently for a few moments, and then went on fervently: "Bless you. *Bless* you!" She jumped away, slammed the door, and ran, waiting for cars to pass. He watched her moving with most attractive ease, and marvelled. Then he saw her waving at a taxi, and saw the taxi slow down.

"Lucky Pamela," he said aloud.

She probably *did* know how lucky she was to be alive.

Certainly he knew how lucky he was, too, but — he did not understand the situation at all. Why try to kill him? Why follow him and the girl to the airport? He had another feeling, which made him shiver; he must have been followed but he hadn't noticed the motor-cyclist until he had pulled the car up here. Once he had the girl, he had not even troubled to keep a look-out. On such an affair as this, he must not be even momentarily careless twice.

Why —

There was no point in asking himself that question, but he simply had to find out. And there were only two ways in which to do so. One, through Pamela Brown whose address was imprinted on his mind from the envelopes in her handbag; the other, through Thomas G. Loman. He sat back, feeling bleak and grim, and it passed through his mind that he had not even got out to examine the damage to the car.

He got out.

At least a dozen dents showed, and two places where the metal was actually jagged; that made him tighten his lips ... Two minutes later when tall, lanky, fair-haired Alex Paterson came up with another detective and the youth, the sight of the jagged edges of metal torn by pieces which had been flung into the air by the bomb made their lips tighten, too.

"That was a hand grenade," he remarked.

"Yes," Rollison said. "These gentry will stop at nothing, will they?"

"What do you know about these gentry, Mr. Rollison?" asked Paterson.

"They appear to be able to operate on both sides of the Atlantic," Rollison answered. "And those on this side are deadly. That is absolutely all I know, although I hope to learn much more." He looked grimly into Paterson's face and went on: "In fact I am going to. Has Loman come round yet?"

"No," answered Paterson.

Rollison looked at him steadily, pondered, and asked: "How soon can we make sure no one throws a hand grenade at him?"

"My *God!*" breathed Paterson. He swung round to his car, picked up the radio telephone, and gave instructions.

Throughout all this, the young man with the piercing blue eyes watched Rollison intently, and now Rollison turned towards him, thinking absurdly: Baby Blue Eyes. There was a baffled look in those eyes, which were a most remarkable blue, and Rollison had an impression that he was suffering from shock.

"May I know your name?" asked Rollison.

"Eh? Oh. Yes, of course. Fisher. Jack Fisher. I — I can't get over what you did and what happened. You — "

"Mr. Fisher," Rollison interrupted, "what time do you come off duty?"

"Oh. Four o'clock, I'm on early turn."

"I'd very much like to talk to you when you're free," Rollison said. "Perhaps we could have a drink."

"At *your* place?"

"Yes, of course."

"The place with the trophies?" asked Jack Fisher, and then apparently he realised he was being naive, and straightened up. "I'd like that very much, sir. I live in Fulham so I'm not very far away from you."

"Shall we say five o'clock?" suggested Rollison. "The address is on the card."

"Five o'clock," said Baby Blue Eyes. "On the dot. I'll look forward to it enormously."

Paterson came away from the car at that moment, while the man with him began to pick up pieces of metal from the ground; only then did Rollison notice that the man had cleared the dirt and grass off the windscreen. There were three chips in the glass, obviously caused by metal fragments, but no other damage. Paterson glanced at this and said:

"When they say safety glass they mean safety."

"Yes," Rollison said, heavily. "Can you have this cleaned up for me?"

"I'll fix it. You just leave the keys," Paterson promised. "Get in my car, will you?"

His was a Morris 1800, and Rollison got in next to the driver's seat, heard Paterson give instructions to his solitary man, and then saw another carload of policemen arrive. Paterson did not wait to talk to them but joined Rollison and started off. He kept silent until they were through the tunnel and on the way to a small group of buildings between two of the main terminals. The red cross denoting First Aid was at one driveway and they turned into this. As he swung into a parking place, Paterson said:

"I talked to Grice, at the Yard."

"Good."

"You don't mind?"

"Why should I?" asked Rollison. "Does he still think I know more than I've admitted about this affair?"

"I got that impression," Paterson answered, coming to a standstill. He had to move his bony knees to one side in order to get them clear of the dashboard: moving, he was an ungainly man. "And when I told him there had been an attempt to murder you, he asked me to make sure you're protected — he'll send a couple of men to take over from mine, Mr. Rollison."

This meant that Rollison was going to be followed wherever he went.

"Everyone is being most considerate," he observed drily. "It may be hard to believe, but I'm more interested in seeing Thomas G. Loman than I am in hearing how worried everyone is about me."

He flashed a smile, and Paterson laughed.

There were two men at the entrance to the two-storey hospital building and another just inside, and when Rollison and Paterson went into a narrow passage off the main one, another man was at the swing doors. At least, the danger was being taken seriously. Paterson led the way, pushing open a door marked 'Private' and Rollison found himself in a small, square, green-painted hospital ward with one bed.

On this, his feet thrusting out at the foot, was a man who lay on his back, with his eyes closed and nothing, at this distance, to suggest that he was alive.

6

Thomas G. Loman?

IN ONE CORNER of the room a small man sat, with a pocket book in his hands. He stood up slowly, gaze fixed on Paterson, who was looking at the bare feet, which were almost at right-angles from the heels. From this angle the toes, particularly the big toe, looked huge. A nurse pushed her way past Rollison and lifted the blanket which draped over the bony ankles, pulled it down and placed it over the feet. It covered them from the top but gave them no real protection. But it was warm in here.

"I told you to watch his feet," the nurse said.

The small man did not answer.

"All right, nurse, thanks," said Paterson, and he looked at the small man. "Has he moved, Jones?"

"Only his feet," said Jones. "It seems like a reflex action to me."

"Has he said anything?"

"Every now and again he gives a kind of snore," announced Jones.

"What is a 'kind' of snore?"

"It's a gulp, really," answered Jones. "I can't really explain, but — oh! There's one coming!"

Exactly what happened, Rollison could not tell. Some kind of muscular contortion appeared to take place in the tall man's midriff, his chest heaved, and he gave a gasping sound, something between a yawn and a groan; this was emitted through his mouth, which closed again immediately.

"You see," said Jones, in triumph.

"How often has he done this?"

"Six times, now," the small man answered precisely.

"I should say he's coming round," Paterson suggested, and turned to Rollison. "Wouldn't you say so?"

"It could be," replied Rollison non-commitally.

"Have you ever seen him before?" asked Paterson.

That was his key question, of course, and the one which Grice wanted answered, and the answer was easy to give. Yet Rollison did not immediately give it. He went closer to the bed, and placed a thumb on the man's left eyelid, raising it. The eye was hazel coloured, the pupil small but not a pin point size. Rollison turned back and said:

"No, I have never seen him before any time anywhere."

"Why did you have to look into his eyes, to find out?"

"I didn't," said Rollison. "I looked into his eye to see whether he was conscious. I don't think he is or he would have started when I first touched it and the eyelid would have flickered. But I doubt if he'll be unconscious for long, now. What did he have with him?"

"Passport, a few coins and small change, some keys and his ticket copy with some baggage receipts clipped on and having your name and address as his address in England," stated Paterson. "Either his luggage was left behind in Tucson, Arizona, or it was stolen, for he didn't have any when he reached New York."

"Oh," said Rollison blankly.

Then a youthful Pakistani doctor came in, was pleasant, examined the patient, assured them that he would come round within an hour, and ushered all of them out, except Jones. It was a very convincing exertion of authority and could cause offence to no one. The nurse pulled the bedclothes down farther over the big feet, but did not even make a pretence of tucking them in. Rollison and Paterson walked past the guard and out to the guards at the front of the small building.

"Have you noticed anything at all suspicious?" asked Paterson.

"No, sir. And we are in regular walkie-talkie contact with the men on either side."

"Don't let anyone on a motor-cycle go in, whatever his credentials," warned Paterson, and then added to Rollison: "His clothes, shoes and everything he had with him are in my office. Fingerprints and Photography will have finished with them by now. Would you care to look at them before I send them to the hospital?"

"Very much," Rollison said.

A few minutes afterwards he was looking at a well-made suit in a sandy-colour, a large-brimmed hat with a curly brim of a darker colour, more brown than sandy, and cowboy boots of the same colour as the hat, beautifully made in a patterned leather. The heels were a different shape from ordinary walking shoes, and the tops were wide and trimmed with darker leather. They had a new look, but were obviously broken in; the leather was soft and pliable. Next to these were a checked shirt with piping at the collar and the two breast pockets, a tie which was like a leather shoelace threaded through what looked like a cow's face in copper and with a turquoise blue filigree ring. The other oddments were impersonal, even to a pack of paper handkerchiefs.

"No socks?" asked Rollison.

"They must have left them at the hospital," Paterson said. "Do you know — " he broke off, as if embarrassed, but when Rollison did not push him to go on, he said:

"This is the first murder attempt I've come across at the airport."

"I wish I knew the motive," Rollison sighed.

Paterson's eyes widened. He had very fair hair and fair skin, and his face was full of freckles.

"Surely that's obvious."

"Tell me, then," begged Rollison.

"To prevent you from seeing him!"

"Oh," said Rollison, startled. "Yes. Yes, possibly."

All the time he had been expecting Paterson to ask questions about the girl who had been with him, but the policeman still did not mention her. The motor-cyclist's attack could have been on her, not on the Toff, but if Jack Fisher had forgotten to mention Pamela Brown then Paterson probably did not know she had been in the car with him. Paterson looked at him curiously and said:

"I would have thought you'd realise that."

"No one wants to believe he's a target for murder," Rollison murmured. "What are you planning to do with Thomas G.?"

"Loman? I'm blessed if I know."

"He did have my address," Rollison mused. "And in view of all that's happened, I'd better take him in. Can you send me an escort car?"

"Grice may have something to say about where he goes," demurred Paterson. "He's sending two men, remember?"

"I remember," Rollison said. "I think you'll find they would like to have me in the West End together with Loman, so that they can keep an eye on our comings and goings. I wonder if you can check on my car?"

His Bristol was battered, it proved, but washed and serviceable.

An hour later, Thomas G. Loman was conscious, and in two hours, the Pakistani doctor said it was all right for him to travel. All Loman could tell the police, it seemed, was that he had fallen asleep in his seat and remembered nothing until he had come round in the hospital.

He still looked dazed.

Meanwhile, Grice's men, a detective sergeant and a detective officer whom Rollison did not know even by sight, had come to take over from Paterson's officers. They were obviously more pleased than sorry that they could go back to London at once. The only piece of information they could give Rollison was negative: there was no trace of the motor-cyclist.

No one else seemed to be aware of the existence of Pamela Brown.

It was half past twelve when Thomas G. Loman, fully dressed, almost unbelievably tall, came out of the hospital, with the nurse by his side. She barely reached his shoulder. Paterson and his men as well as the two men from the Yard were watching, obviously intent on finding out if Loman showed any sign of recognition.

Rollison, standing by the side of his car, said:

"I'm Richard Rollison."

The other hesitated; this puzzled Rollison, who thought there was a question in his mind; but he did not put it into words.

"Shall we go?" Rollison suggested.

"Sure." Loman immediately moved towards the driving wheel, but then drew back, gaping. "The wheel's on the wrong side!"

"We do things that way in England," Rollison explained.

"England? Oh — of course." In a few long strides the American went to the other side, opened the door and climbed in; he showed the tall man's care in bending his knees and stretching his legs. He put them out at full length and looked round in astonishment. "There's good room," he said. "Is that the way you do things in England, too?"

"Only when a car is custom-built," said Rollison.

"*Gee!*" breathed Thomas G. Loman.

He appeared then to surrender himself wholly to the joy of the car; its upholstery, its comfort, its instruments, its smooth starting, its easy riding. He leaned back in his seat and half closed his eyes and appeared to be ecstatic. Then he sat up and bumped his head.

"Oh!"

"And *that's* the way we do things in England," Rollison said. "Be careful."

"I certainly will," promised his passenger.

He began to look about him as if for the first time. He stared at cars and stared at people, at houses and the shops. Now and again he rubbed his long fingers together; he could make a cracking sound with his knuckles. Rollison did not try to make him talk yet; he was bound to ask questions before long, and information would probably come easier that way.

"Gee," he said, "it's different."

"Very different?" asked Rollison.

"Oh, sure, different. There's so much green," observed Loman. "And all of the cars are so small. And a lot of people walk."

"Don't they in Tucson?" asked Rollison.

"Only down town — say, this isn't London yet, is it?"

"We're on the outskirts."

"I will say one thing," said Loman after a pause. "Everything sure is green." He edged up in his seat and looked about him for a long time, and then declared "It sure is green."

"We get a lot of rain," remarked Rollison, solemnly.

"Rain," echoed Loman, and added: "Sure. We get ours in July and December."

Rollison wondered how long it would be before the man began to explain; there was no great hurry as far as he could judge, and it may even have to wait until they reached Gresham Terrace. He had not called Jolly, so Jolly would have lunch ready. He glanced in the driving mirror, and saw the police car. He would be followed wherever he went until the mystery was solved or unless he gave his shadowers the slip. There was no need to do that yet. He passed the end of Hood Lane, and half-smiled at the thought of Pamela Brown, who certainly hadn't told all she knew. Behind that sweet and innocent façade and ingenuousness of manner was a sharp and undoubtedly devious mind. An M.G. not unlike hers passed in the opposite direction, with a man at the wheel.

"Excuse me," Loman said.

"Yes," said Rollison promptly.

"I didn't get your name."

"You didn't — " began Rollison, and actually took his eyes off the road to look sharply at the American. But Loman was now sitting back, eyes half-closed, a dreamy smile on his face. He had a remarkable profile, a face half as long again as an average face but everything in proportion; his eyes were deep and seemed to push his cheekbones down. His upper lip was long, and so was his chin; in profile it did not seem to be so spade-shaped.

Unless he was very clever at dissembling, this young man meant exactly what he said: he had not caught Rollison's name.

Rollison drew in a deep breath.

"My name is Richard Rollison," he stated carefully. "Of 25g, Gresham Terrace."

Loman began to frown. Out of the corner of his eyes Rollison saw him glance towards him, a quick, appraising glance. He sat even more upright in his seat, and after a while said:

"Richard Rallison."

"Rollison."

"Row-lisson."

"There are two ells, which make the 'o' short," explained Rollison, and pronounced his name again with great care. Traffic was now very thick and he needed to concentrate on driving, so dared not look at the American who had now twisted round in his seat and was staring, much as Pamela Brown had earlier.

Very slowly and deliberately, he said:

"Rol-liss-on."

"That's it," approved Rollison. "That's exactly right. Richard Rollison."

"Then," stated Thomas G. Loman, "you are the man I've come to see."

"That's what it said on your aeroplane ticket as I understand it," Rollison agreed. "When the police discovered that, and also discovered that you had been given a shot of morphine and afterwards robbed, they asked if I would come and see you. That's why I'm here."

They were now out of the various overpasses and in Cromwell Road, with the tall, old-fashioned terraced houses on either side. Traffic was very thick, the stench of fumes nauseating on a warm English autumn day. A huge B.E.A. coach pushed by, crowding Rollison; the car behind him hooted. It wasn't the police car, which had fallen farther behind. Soon, they were in thinner traffic by the Kensington museums, but a thick bottleneck at the approach to Knightsbridge lay ahead.

"Mr. Rollison," Loman said, suddenly: "Is this London?"

"Yes — this is near the heart of London."

"Those are pretty big buildings on the left."

"They are museums. We are just entering Knightsbridge, one of the several centres of London." Rollison found himself talking like a tour guide, and even enthusing over London. Unless the traffic was slowed down to a crawl in Piccadilly they would be in Gresham Terrace in ten minutes, and this was neither time nor place to start a game of questions and answers. It crossed his mind that Loman might open the door and get out when they were at a standstill, but the young American showed no sign of doing that. Indeed, he marvelled.

"That's sure bigger than Levy's," he said of Harrods.

"Levy's?"

"That's the biggest department store in Tucson. That place is bigger. Har-rods." He looked about him at thronged pavements, shops and tall buildings, and was startled when they drove beneath the Hyde Park Underpass. As they came up in Piccadilly he said: "Gee! That park has more trees than Randolph, and it sure is green. You must have a lot of rain in England."

"We have enough," Rollison said, wryly. He put on his blinker for the next left hand turn, since Gresham Terrace was now only a few hundred yards away. He made the turn, with Thomas G. Loman still looking about him. Then Loman straightened up as Rollison said: "We'll be at my home in two or three minutes."

"That's fine," said Loman. "I am surely looking forward to seeing an English home, Mr. Rollison." He put a slightly exaggerated emphasis on the 'Roll' but otherwise pronounced the name well. "Would you mind answering me a question? Would you mind telling me why you asked me to come and see you? Because I sure would like to know."

7

Dead End

"MR. LOMAN," ROLLISON SAID, somehow holding on to his patience. "What are you called? Tom or Thomas or Tommy or what?"

"Tom," answered Loman, calmly. The fact that Rollison had so parried his question did not seem to affect him at all. "Just Tom. What do they call you? Richard? Or Dick? Or Dickie?"

Rollison shuddered.

"Never Dickie," he replied. "Seldom Dick. Often Richard. Much more often, Rolly."

"Like in holly?" asked Loman.

"Exactly as in holly."

"Thanks."

They were in Gresham Terrace, and by one of the near miracles that can make or mar a modern day, a parking space loomed up only a few yards from Number 25. Rollison manoeuvred the car into it, inches from the kerb, and Loman uncoiled himself and got out. He stood at his full height, peering up at the tall, graceful buildings, and slowly shook his head.

"I've never seen any place like it," he declared.

"Except for a few dozen streets about here, there aren't any," Rollison told him. "There's one grave disadvantage. There is no lift."

"Come again."

"No lift — no *elevator*."

"You mean you walk up? Like in a New York brown-stone?"

"Yes. And I live on the top floor."

"If there's one thing I have learned about you," volunteered Thomas G. Loman. "It's that you like doing things the hard way." He looked up and down the street again, seeing the great variety of parked cars and a dozen people including a nursemaid holding a toddler by the hand, and then he actually patted the roof of the car. "What do you call her?" he asked.

"A nurse," answered Rollison, with resignation.

Loman looked astonished. "You call her — " he broke off, and smiled.

He had half-smiled before, just showing his white teeth set in the angular lower jaw, but this was the first time Rollison had really seen him smile as if he were deeply amused. It created deep lines at his eyes and others at the corners of his mouth, and it sank his jaw inches lower than its norm. Also, it wrinkled his nose at either side; there was no doubt at all that it made him look remarkably like a horse; a happy horse, Rollison thought with helpless indulgence.

"I don't mean the blonde," he said. "I mean the automobile!"

"Oh, the Bristol."

"Come again."

"The Bristol. B-R-I-"

"I know how you spell the name of the maker," interrupted Loman. "You don't have a name for her?"

"No."

"I thought all the British had a name for their auto-mobiles. Like Genevieve, or something."

"Genevieve — " began Rollison, and then he laughed outright. "Did you see the film of the old crocks' race?"

"I surely did, answered Loman. "It was a dandy. So you don't have a name for this beauty?"

"I'm afraid not," Rollison said.

Loman shrugged, and they turned into the door of the house where Rollison lived. The tall American had to duck to get beneath the lintel, and once inside, stood and gaped up the narrow well of the staircase and the narrow staircase itself, with its wrought iron balustrade and the purple carpet. He held on to the rail as he went up ahead of the Toff, paused at each half and each main landing to look down, reached the landing before the Toff's and stood still.

"Why don't you find a name for your car?"

Rollison said amiably: "If you really want me to, I'll consider it."

"Sure, I want you to. An automobile like that shouldn't be anonymous. Mr. — Rolly. Will you tell me something?"

Rollison thought: He can't put the subject off much longer, and said: "Yes."

"What happened to your automobile?" asked Loman.

"In what way do you mean?"

"The holes. The dents. The gashes. Boy, they certainly made that automobile of heavy grade steel, any ordinary auto would have been like a pepper pot. It didn't happen long ago, the edges where big pieces of metal tore through the steel are bright as silver. No oxidisation. So — what happened to the Bristol, Mr. — Richard?"

Rollison started up the stairs, but suddenly Loman gripped his arm with powerful fingers, and unless he wanted a struggle, it would be folly to pull himself free.

He saw the front door of his flat open an inch and had no doubt that Jolly was behind it, listening: he would have wondered why they were taking so long getting upstairs.

"A youth on a motor-cycle threw a hand grenade, but missed the window," Rollison said clearly. "It struck the ground and went off: the Bristol caught most of the splinters."

The door opened wider, an indication of Jolly's concern.

Thomas G. Loman's mouth dropped open and he took his hand away.

"*Today?*" he asked.

"Today."

"In *Eng*land?"

"At London Airport," Rollison asseverated.

Thomas G. Loman blinked, closed his mouth and gulped, then slowly shook his head and said in a hopeless-sounding voice: "England is a surprising country. It sure is." He started up the stairs again, still shaking his head — until Jolly opened the door wider still, showing his concern.

They were at the top landing.

Loman looked at Jolly as if at an apparition: the black jacket, grey cravat, striped trousers and highly polished black shoes. The sparse grey hair, too, and lined face. The melancholy brown eyes were turned towards Rollison and not until he was satisfied that his employer was unhurt did he acknowledge Loman, inclining his head and saying:

"Good afternoon, sir."

"Jolly," Rollison said. "Mr. Loman will be staying with us for a few days. And meanwhile, if lunch hasn't spoiled — " He paused hopefully.

"Will ten minutes be all right, sir?"

"Perfect," said Rollison. "You look after things in the kitchen, I'll take Mr. Loman to his room."

Jolly went the back way, Rollison led Loman into the study-cum-living room and saw him rake the Trophy Wall with his gaze. They both paused for a few moments, not saying a word, before Rollison led the way by the other passage to the spare room. This was small, but had a large bed across which even a man of six feet six could sprawl. Rollison saw at a glance that Jolly had cleared away the usual vanities and accessories that delighted a woman and had put out a set of silver backed brushes and silver combs. Some leather containers were there for masculine needs, and Jolly had placed the day's newspapers as well as the latest *Time* and *Playboy* on the bedside table.

Loman appeared to take all this in at a glance, then turned and looked down at Rollison from his great height and demanded in an unbelieving voice:

"Did you call him *Jolly*, Rolly?"

He stood there determinedly bewildered. His mouth opened half an inch and the expression in his eyes reminded Rollison of Pamela Brown's. There was something so helpless-seeming about him that, whether it was deceptive or not, Rollison felt the kind of sympathy he would feel for a young calf which had strayed from its mother. The spontaneous chuckle which had overtaken him several times today bubbled up and over, but not until he had said:

"Yes. Yes and — it's not supposed to be funny." He gave a snort of laughter but won only bafflement from Tom Loman. "He — he has been with me since before I was your age," he managed to say.

"You mean he's a family *retainer*?"

"You could say that," Rollison agreed.

"Family retainers and jet aircraft, airport bombings and a man who doesn't turn a hair at any kind of danger. Are you sure this is England, Rolly? Not Alice-in-Wonderland or something out of Hogarth?"

"Not Alice nor the eighteenth century," Rollison assured him. "The bathroom's through that doorway. Can you be ready in five minutes?"

"Sure can," Loman assured him. He studied Rollison deliberately then shot out his long arms and dropped his hands on Rollison's shoulders with the now familiar powerful grip, and went on in a deeper voice: "And after we've eaten we just have to talk. And I mean talk."

"We shall talk," Rollison promised, faintly.

Five minutes later, Loman entered the big room by the rear passage, a little ahead of Rollison. He went straight to the fireplace, just then screened, and surveyed the Trophy Wall. In fact he did not move until Rollison appeared; even then, he only moved his eyes.

"Will you have a drink?" asked Rollison.

"I guess not," answered Loman. "Mr. Rollison, am I correct in believing that collection is unique?"

"I think it probably is," Rollison said.

"I'm darned sure it is," said Loman, with a surge of vigour. "I read about that, somewhere. I don't remember much about it but I remember reading about that wall." He saw Jolly appear from the other direction, carrying a steaming dish, and was soon at the hotplate near the table, helping himself to stewed beef which had been cooked very slowly in a red wine and flavoured with delicate spices that gave it a rare aroma and delicious savour. He finished long before the Toff, who jumped up, took his plate, and said:

"Let me get you some more."

Loman took a second helping, ate somewhat more slowly, and shook his head sorrowfully when offered a third. As Jolly was bringing in a crisp-looking open apple tart and some whipped cream, he said:

"Did you cook that, Mr. Jolly?"

"That was my pleasure, sir."

"You want to know something?" Loman asked. "At any hotel or restaurant in Tucson, you could make a fortune."

Jolly kept a wholly straight face.

"That is very gracious of you, sir, but I am very happy where I am."

"In London?" asked Loman.

"Yes indeed, sir. Will you have —?"

"It's always warm in Tucson."

"I am sure it is a delightful place, sir, but when one is getting on in years one moves from the familiar only with great reluctance."

"Mr. Jolly," announced Loman. "Tucson is just the place for you. It's full of senior citizens."

"Of *what*, sir?"

"Senior citizens. Old folk who — "

"You must forgive me, sir," said Jolly, very firmly, "but I am doubtful whether I should like Tucson."

"Not like Tucson!"

"No, sir. I — "

"Everybody likes Tucson!"

"Sir," said Jolly, standing with the tart in one hand and a silver slice in the other, "with the greatest respect, I do not believe that I would enjoy a temperature of a hundred and five to a hundred and fifteen, which I understand is common in summer. Moreover I like some humidity, and I understand that the humidity in Tucson except during the summer heat is not high. I am moreover allergic to certain pollens and dust irritates the membranes of my nose and throat. Further, with a few exceptions the buildings are of one or two storeys only, I understand, and I enjoy heights. Moreover — "

"Rolly," said Loman, in a sharp voice, "how come your man knows so much about Tucson?"

"He knows much more than I do," Rollison conceded.

"When I heard that Mr. Rollison was going to meet you at the airport I consulted the encyclopaedia," stated Jolly. "Further, I talked to a friend in Thomas Cooks and he was good enough to send me a brochure on Tucson and Southern Arizona. It is fascinating, sir, but not for me." Jolly left this statement hanging for at least twenty seconds, and only when it was at last obvious that Loman was too flabbergasted to reply did he ask: "Will you have cream with the apple tart, sir? Or would you prefer cheese?"

"Cream," Loman answered huskily.

Rollison caught Jolly's eye as Jolly went out; they were brimming over with merriment. Loman's were not; they were brimming over with something which might have been yearning. He forked a piece of the apple tart and cream, placed it in his mouth, and the only word to describe his expression was 'reverence'. When he had finished, he said, still huskily:

"In the right place, Mr. Jolly would be worth a million dollars."

"You must tell him so," said Rollison.

"I believe he would listen to you before he would listen to me," commented Loman, with obvious regret. He scraped up the last morsel and pushed back his chair. His expression changed; he took on a bleak look at mouth and eyes and stared intently at Rollison.

"You sent for me and now you're giving me the brush off," he said. "I want to know why."

"I did not send for you. Until today I had never heard

of you, and I am giving you the courtesy I would normally give to a guest," replied Rollison.

Silence fell upon them.

Jolly came into the room with coffee on a tray but he did not speak, simply placed the coffee on a small table in the main part of the room, and withdrew. Neither of the others appeared to have noticed him.

"Mr. Rollison," Thomas Loman said, "one of us is lying, and I know it isn't me. I want to know the truth right now." He raised his large, well-shaped hands, so powerful looking, and crooked the strong, lean fingers. "If you won't give it me straight, I'll have to force it out of you. I'll give you one more chance. Why did you send for me? Why did you write and tell me that if I came at once, it would be worth a million pounds — not dollars, pounds?"

He pushed his chair farther back and stood looming over the Toff, unquestioningly menacing, hands still thrust forward and fingers crooked..

8

" . . . Pounds not Dollars"

A GREAT DEAL HAD HAPPENED to Rollison that day. He
had been woken out of deep sleep to answer a call about
this man of whom he had never heard. The incident of
Pamela Brown had been amusing and yet exasperating,
the attitude of William Grice had been annoying, and
the attack at the airport had, he knew, a delayed action
shock effect. It was a combination of all these things
which had worked in him to make him keep his com-
posure: until now.

Suddenly, he felt a blaze of anger.

He had to fight back the impulse to jump to his feet
and get his blow in first. Angry though he was, he was
aware that Loman was very powerful and at least fifteen
years younger than he.

"Sit down," he barked.

Loman leaned farther forward.

"You are going to tell me, or — " he began.

Rollison shot out his right hand, gripped a bony wrist
at the vital spot, and twisted. Taken entirely by surprise,
Loman went staggering backwards and thumped against
the wall. Rollison rounded the table and stood in front of
the younger man, who began to slide helplessly down the
wall, losing height rapidly.

"Now behave like a rational human being or get out,"

Rollison said coldly. "The rest of this affair is bad enough without having you behaving like an ill-bred bull."

He stared icily upon his guest, then turned and went into the Trophy Room, where Jolly had appeared as if by magic. He gave an almost imperceptible shake of his head, saying in effect: "Leave this to me," and poured out coffee. Jolly hovered, out of Loman's sight. Rollison was aware that the young American was standing upright again but had no ideas what his mood would be like.

Loman stepped down from the dining alcove as the telephone bell rang. Rollison moved like a flash to the desk, plucked up the telephone, and announced: "Rollison." Immediately, a man responded.

"That *is* Mr. Rollison?"

"Yes," said Rollison.

"You — er — you *did* invite me to come and have a drink about five o'clock this afternoon, didn't you?" the caller went on. "I — er — I wasn't dreaming."

"I'd very much like you to come."

"Then I'll be there, as soon as I can be. Oh! This is Jack Fisher, the man who saw the explosion this morning."

"I remember you very well," Rollison said.

"Do you know if they've caught the men yet?" asked Fisher, and added in a voice touched as if with horror: "To try to kill you — why, it's criminal!"

In spite of himself, Rollison chuckled. "Yes, isn't it? Soon after five, then." He replaced the receiver and turned round slowly, not sure how near Loman was yet acutely aware of him. If this really came to a conflict he must finish it very quickly.

Loman stood like a big boy with a slightly hangdog air.

"I'm sorry," he said simply.

"If we have to tangle with each other, let's make sure

it's for a good reason," said Rollison. "Help yourself to
sugar and cream." He stood with his back to the fireplace, cup in hand. After lunch Jolly always served tall,
slender cups; after dinner, *demi-tasses*. "Have you got
this letter which was supposed to be from me?"

"No," answered Loman. "All my baggage was stolen
on the flight from Tucson to New York. And nearly
everything else was stolen on the B.O.A.C flight."

"You mean they robbed you *twice*?"

"They surely did. And I was doped twice, too."

"Oh," said Rollison slowly. "It looks as if they didn't
find what they wanted in the baggage, and had a second
go." He moved quickly, lifted the telephone, dialled the
number of Scotland Yard, asked for Grice and was prepared to have to leave a message. But Grice himself
answered. "Bill," Rollison said. "Loman was doped and
robbed on his Flight — number?" he asked Loman.

"Flight 212, TWA."

"Flight 212, TWA," Rollison passed on to Grice. "He
was given a shot on that aircraft, too, so it's possible the
same man or woman did the two jobs. Is there a way of
checking the two passenger lists?"

"As far as we can judge, Loman was the only passenger
who was on both flights. All the others who left the aircraft at Kennedy have been traced by New York," Grice
responded. "But whoever it was probably didn't use the
same name. I'll check, though. Has Loman been able to
explain?"

"He says I wrote to him and told him that if he came
to see me I would arrange for him to get one million
pounds — pounds, not dollars," Rollison added for
emphasis. "He doesn't really want to believe that I didn't
write to him at all, but I think he's come round to it. Have
you had any luck?"

"The bomb was an English World War II hand

grenade," Grice announced. "We haven't a line on the motor-cyclist yet, I'm afraid. Rolly — " He paused.

"Yes, Bill?"

"Don't hold any morning mood against me, will you?"

Rollison chuckled. "No, William, I will not!" He rang off, feeling remarkably high-spirited although there was a warning note in his mind: vacillations in his own mood had to be watched, he needed to unwind. He moved back to the fireplace and explained: "That was Chief Superintendant Grice of Scotland Yard. He started the day like a Doubting Thomas, too. Thomas — "

"Richard," said Loman. "I have told you everything I can."

"Not everything. When did you get the letter, for instance?"

"Last Friday," stated Loman.

"Only five days ago?"

"I couldn't move any faster," said Loman, apologetically. "All the banks were closed when I got the letter, so I couldn't get money or travellers cheques. A friend brought the letter out to the ranch from Tucson for me."

"Where is the letter?" asked Rollison.

"It was in my grip," replied Loman, "which means I may have seen the last of it. I would have come sooner but I had to buy some clothes and make arrangements with my boss to have my job back if this turned out to be fool's gold."

"So you thought it might be," Rollison said.

"Sure," Thomas answered laconically. "But I always wanted to visit England. My folks were said to come from England, a place called Stratford-on-Avon, maybe you know it. So I bought me a suit and got me some money — "

"How much money did you lose on the trip?"

"One thousand dollars in cash money and five thousand

in travellers cheques," Loman answered. "I left one thousand dollars in the bank in case I got home hungry." Loman gave his slow, lazy grin. "They left me my billfold on Flight 212, it wasn't until the second flight they took that. I guess I'm broke."

"Do you have the numbers of those travellers cheques?"

"In the billfold," Loman answered.

"You can call American Express and tell them where you bought them and get them cancelled," Rollison said. "They'll replace them in London when they learn what's happened. Do you know what the thieves were after?"

"No, sir. Unless it was the letter."

"Where *was* that letter?"

"In my billfold."

"Our word for billfold is wallet," Rollison told him. "Were there any other papers?"

"Yes, sir," answered Loman.

"What?"

"My birth certificate, I guess."

"Ah! Did I ask for that?"

"You sure did."

"And more?"

"Sure," answered Loman. "Some old papers showing my grandpa had come from Stratford-on-Avon, a kind of family tree, I guess."

"Wasn't that in the baggage?"

"No, sir."

"In your hand baggage — anything that was stolen in New York?"

"No, sir," repeated Loman. "I kept those papers in an envelope in my pocket, I didn't want to take any chances with them. You think that's what the thieves were after?"

"I think it could have been," answered Rollison

slowly, and he went on, hardly daring to ask: "Have you any copies of these documents?"

"No," answered Loman. "Why would I want copies when I have the genuine article?"

"Some people play safe," Rollison remarked heavily. "Were you carrying anything else in your pockets?"

"I guess not — I got everything else back at the airport."

Rollison asked, out of the blue: "What was your grandfather's name?"

"Joseph."

"Joseph what?"

"Joseph Loman, what else?"

"It could have been on your mother's side," Rollison pointed out. "Did you —?"

"There was something else!" cried Loman. It did not occur to him to wait but whenever a thought came into his head he interrupted in the most natural way. "I'd forgotten, I guess. There were some old photographs."

"Of you?"

"Are you crazy? Of my grandfather and his wife. They were pretty old, those brown-coloured prints, what do you call them? Sepia, that's the word, sepia. I've had them ever since my pa handed them to me just before he died. Had them in a special folder," Tommy Loman added. "It was too big for my billfold so I put them in this envelope so they could all go into my pocket." His eyes glowed with this happy recollection, but the Toff's heart sank.

"Tommy," he said.

"Yes?"

"Do you have any brothers?"

"No, sir. No brothers, no sisters."

"Cousins?" asked Rollison.

"I've never heard of any relatives any place," answered Loman.

"No one at all like you?"

"Richard," stated Loman with great certainty, "there ain't nobody like me, any place."

"I can believe it," Rollison replied feelingly, and he moved towards the tall man, going on in an even voice. "Tommy, I am only guessing but it looks to me like a good guess. You appear to stand to inherit a lot of money — that's the simple and obvious explanation. If someone wants to prevent you from getting it, then the obvious means would be to impersonate you. That could be done safely only by killing you or keeping you out of the way until the inheritance had been claimed and paid over. The simple way would be to kill you but not until they had these documents and photographs. From now on, if I'm anywhere on course, so far as these impersonators are concerned you would be far better dead."

The word 'dead' hovered about the room and seemed to echo from the trophies on that resplendent wall. As it hovered, Rollison looked into Tommy Loman's light brown eyes. The younger man's face was blank, he looked almost as if he had not taken in everything that Rollison said.

But he had taken it in, for he said: "It would make sense, I guess, if you had written and told me about a legacy. But you didn't. So who did? And who told me to come see you?"

"That we shall find out."

"And who tried to blow you up?" asked Loman. "*You*, Richard, not me."

"We shall find that out, too," Rollison promised. "We have found out one thing: you are in danger."

After a long pause, Loman said: "So?"

"So, we must look after you."

"I'm good at looking after myself," Loman retorted laconically.

"On a cattle ranch, I am sure you are. But in an aeroplane?" Loman opened his mouth to reply, but closed it again. "Or in London, a strange city where you don't even know the rule of the road?"

Resignedly, the other said: "So how are you going to protect me?"

"In the first place, have you stay here," Rollison began. "Then — "

"Richard," interrupted Loman, spreading his hands, "do you know what claustrophobia is? Do you know what it feels like to be in a big city surrounded by bricks and stone when you're accustomed to riding a range where all you can see are mountains and saguaro cacti and dirt?"

"I can imagine," Rollison conceded.

"This is a nice room," stated Loman. "But."

"It won't be for ever," Rollison said.

"It can't be for long, Richard. And there's another thing."

"What's that?"

"When I'm in trouble I like to do my own protecting."

"Yes," Rollison said levelly. "Yes, I am sure you do. However, you must stay here the rest of the day and tonight, at least. I may be able to find out what's really behind all this if I have a little time. At seven o'clock we shall have company — " He called across to Jolly, who was clearing the table. "Did I tell you that Miss Brown will be here for dinner, Jolly?"

"No, sir," Jolly replied, and straightened up with a crumb tray in one hand, crumb brush in the other. "Then I should go and do a little shopping."

"Hey!" exclaimed Loman, in sudden excitement.

"What's the matter?" demanded Rollison.

"I can go out with Mr. Jolly! He can look after me."
A glint of merriment showed in the tall man's eyes.

"Tommy," Rollison said very softly, "I don't think
you understand. The evidence is that you are in grave
danger. Until we know what kind of danger you need
to take extreme precautions. We know that the people
involved are prepared to throw an explosive grenade,
and if they'll do it once they might again. If you want to
go out and risk your neck, I shan't stop you. But I won't
risk Jolly's. I'm not yet sure it's worth it."

Very slowly and deliberately, Tommy Loman backed
away and at the same time raised his hands.

"I can say one thing about you," he said in a husky
voice. "You speak straight and you act fast. You want me
to stay here that bad?"

"I think you would be wiser to stay here," Rollison
answered.

"Okay, then I'll stay," promised Loman, reluctantly.
"If I change my mind I'll tell you. Are you going to have
the place surrounded?" The amused glint appeared in
his eyes again.

"Yes," answered Rollison.

"Jehosophat!" exclaimed Loman. "You mean it!"

"I mean it," confirmed Rollison, turning to Jolly.
"Call Bill Ebbutt and ask for some of his chaps, Jolly,
then tell Mr. Grice what I've done and why — because
I think Mr. Loman's life is in acute danger."

"And isn't *yours*, sir?" asked Jolly, very earnestly.
"And if it is, isn't it simply because you are helping a
complete stranger, who really has no call on you at all?"

9

The Short and the Tall

ROLLISON DID NOT REPLY but looked at Thomas G. Loman, who actually backed a pace, as if Jolly had delivered him a physical blow. His face showed a whole gamut of expressions, from shock to unbelief; until at last he turned to Rollison and spoke with unmistakable feeling.

"And I said that *you* talk straight."

"When one is dealing with life and death, as Mr. Rollison and I have been for many years, one has to talk very straight indeed," said Jolly.

"Sure," conceded Loman. "You bet!" He flashed his most attractive grin. "I'll be good," he promised. "But if you two go out and leave me alone I don't promise not to prowl around."

"Prowl wherever you like," Rollison said. "Are you going to look for anything in particular?"

"All I can find out about you and Mr. Jolly."

"In the cupboards beneath the Trophy Wall you will find press cuttings books and case histories. Help yourself." Rollison pointed to three cupboards with sliding doors beneath a wide ledge about the height of his desk on the wall, then turned to Jolly. "Show Mr. Loman our safety measures, won't you?" He smiled at Loman and then turned and walked briskly out of the room.

He went to his bedroom and knelt down beside a big wardrobe, opened the doors and then a drawer at the bottom, pressed a knot in the wood at one side and allowed a false bottom to slide back smoothly and with little sound.

Hidden here were weapons in great variety.

He selected a small pistol not unlike the one which Pamela Brown had in her bag, and four cigarettes which he placed carefully into his gold cigarette case. Each cigarette was in fact a tiny blow-pipe and inside it not a dart but a phial of tear gas; that little invention, thought up over twenty years ago, had saved his life times out of number. He picked up a narrow, stiletto dagger clipped into an arm band. This would fit comfortably below the elbow, from where he could work it down towards his hand by flexing his muscles. He put this back again, saying: "Not this jaunt," and left the flat by the other passage, hearing Jolly talking to Tommy G. He glanced up at the periscope mirror and satisfied himself no one was on the staircase or the landing, then went out.

Just outside the street door stood one of Grice's men, another stood on the far side of the street, making no secret of their presence, and returning Rollison's amiable nod. Police protection, Rollison thought half-bleak, half-amused. He saw a third man who did not look like a policeman, farther along the street.

On the instant, he was prepared for trouble.

The man was of medium height, chubby rather than fat, and he wore a pale coloured suit, of a peculiar shade of blue grey. That, and his hat, betrayed him as an American; or at least that he had bought these clothes in America. The man took a step from a wall in front of one of the houses, and Rollison's alarm signals faded; at least the other was not attempting to hide himself.

"Excuse me," the man said, quietly. He was un-mistakably American.

"Can I help you?" Rollison asked.

"Can you — " there was a moment's hesitation before the speaker went on. "Can you tell me where Piccadilly is?"

Rollison was as nearly sure as he could be that his accoster had switched questions at the last moment. He looked into the healthy, olive-skinned complexion and the honey brown eyes as he answered.

"That's very easy. Go along there — " he pointed — "take the first left and then the first left again. It's no more than a hundred yards."

"Thank you," the man said, and turned and walked off.

Rollison got into his car, so pre-occupied that he hardly noticed the dents and holes in the body, eased out of the parking place and went in the opposite direction to that of the American. He did not notice the two detectives, drove by side streets towards Park Lane and finally into Hyde Park, joining a fast-moving stream of traffic. Grice's men were obviously watching both the flat and Loman. Soon, he was driving along the Edgware Road, with its small shops and its crowds, then along a street which was cut in two by a stream of water: the Regent's Canal; for a few hundred yards, the countryside seemed to be in the heart of London. Somehow, the hint of rural England was more impressive here than in the great parks themselves.

And there was room to park!

He sat still for at least three minutes. Several cars passed but no driver or passenger took any notice of him. Some small boys were tossing stones into the Canal, birds darted, two ducks appeared to float by. He got out of the car at last and crossed the road, walked fifty or sixty yards to a house numbered 68. He turned in, walked on to a ramp to the front door, and pressed a bell-push. Almost immediately an elderly woman with the figure of a teenager opened the door.

"Yes?" she said, slightly querulous — and then her expression changed to one of warmth and welcome. "Why, it's Mr. Rollison! Come in, do." She stood aside to allow him to pass in a narrow passage. "Percy will be delighted to see you. He really will!"

She pushed the door open on to a room of photographs; the walls were covered with them, from floor to ceiling, and there were more on filing cabinets and tables. In the window, sat a big, broad-faced man, whose face was lined either from pain or anxiety.

His eyes lit up, and he touched the metal arm of his chair and swung himself round; it was an invalid chair, which he had needed for as many years as Rollison had known him.

His handshake was powerful enough to crush unsuspecting visitors.

"Rolly!"

"Percy."

"You look magnificent!"

"You look as if you're bearing up."

"Just about," roared Percy Bingham. "You're just about right, as usual. Well, now! How can I help you?"

Rollison, sitting in an old-fashioned button-back Victorian sofa, refused a cigarette, and said:

"You can find me an actor, six feet six or seven, lean as a lamp, stands and walks with a slight stoop, has a long, lean face and a spade-like jaw. He must be around twenty-five to thirty years old and able to speak with the accent of a man from the great south west of America."

After a moment's pause, Percy retorted:

"That's a tall order." They both laughed, before Percy asked: "What do you want him for?"

"Probably, attempted murder," Rollison answered.

"*Murder!*" exclaimed the little woman, who came in briskly with a tray holding glasses and a small decanter. This would be cherry brandy, Rollison knew; it was part of the ritual of a meeting of old friends.

"Thank you, sweetheart," Percy said. "Now leave us alone, unless you want to be frightened out of your wits." The smile he gave the woman as she went out was one of deep affection. "What else can you tell me, Rolly?"

"He may be in training to impersonate a man who answers the description I've just given you."

"Well," said Percy Bingham, pouring a little brandy into small, bow-shaped glasses. "I know of only three possibles. Eyes?"

"Honey-coloured."

"I know of only one possible," Percy said, with absolute certainty. "If there is an actor who fits, this is your man. Of course your man may not be an actor."

"I think he is," Rollison said. "Only an actor could do what I think this man is going to do. Can you find out if he's free?"

"Yes, of course." Percy gave a twist to his chair so that he was close to a row of three-drawer filing cabinets, one red, one black, one green. He pulled open the middle drawer in the green cabinet and ran through a number of cards under the letter K. Deftly, he selected one card, glanced at it, then handed it to Rollison while he wheeled himself closer to the telephone and began to dial.

King, Alec George, the card was headed: *Flat 3, Rubicon House, Fell Street, Chelsea, S.W.3.* Rollison knew the narrow street and thought he probably knew the house, too. *Age: 27 (at 1st January 1968). Educated:*

Nelson College. That was a small public school with a liking, obviously, for the sons of sailors.

Training: South Western Repertory Company.

Special suitability: Character acting for very tall, supple man. For tall, read 6 feet 7 inches.

Acting Career. As a child, a number of walk-on parts . . .

There were several short paragraphs about the plays, films and radio he had appeared in and at the foot a note saying: *Photograph and Physical Details: Over.* Rollison flicked it over as Percy began to talk on the telephone. A large face was there, vivid, arresting. This man was like Tommy G. and there were some striking similarities, including the long, spade-shaped chin, the jutting eyebrows. Among the physical details were:

Height:	6′ 7″
Hair:	Fair
Eyes:	Pale brown
Distinguishing marks on face:	None

Rollison put the card aside as Percy replaced the receiver.

"Me first?" he asked, and went on when Rollison nodded: "His wife answered. She says he's in work, what she calls a very important part but they must not say what it is. When I said I might find him work for at least a month she said this present part would go on for a long time. Sound like your man?"

"It could well be," Rollison said. "Percy, you've been invaluable. But then, you always are." He sipped the brandy and they chattered for five minutes before Rollison stood up briskly and said: "I ought to be on the way."

"Don't wait so long before you come again," Percy urged.

He was at his desk near the window when Rollison walked past, hand raised. A breeze set the leaves of the trees rustling, and would give Percy Bingham much pleasure; he had moved to this particular spot only when he had learned that he would never walk again.

Rollison reached his car.

Not long ago, not far from here, someone who had wanted him dead had put high-explosive under the bonnet, set to go off at a touch of the self-starter. It was absurd to think there was a booby trap under the bonnet here, but — well, he would look.

There, fastened to the self-starter, was a small plastic phial.

There, in fact, *was* a bomb.

He stood staring down, a shiver running up and down his spine. People passed, glancing at him. He looked along the street, then down to the canal and the path alongside it. The boys were still tossing stones but the ducks had gone. A car passed, slowly, and he looked up.

A man sitting next to the driver of the car, a Rover, was staring at him. He had a chubby face, a beautiful olive-skin, and fine brown eyes; Rollison had last seen him in Gresham Terrace.

The car gathered speed and went on, and before Rollison could move, other cars were in the roadway. Farther along, he saw a policeman's helmet. He bent closer to see how the plastic container was fastened to the metal, and could see no way.

Suddenly, he realised that it was stuck on; and with a quick-setting glue, that probably meant it was very tight indeed. He straightened up, to find the policeman very close by, a pale-faced weakling of a man to look at.

"Good afternoon, sir."

"Good afternoon," returned Rollison, and forced a smile: "Do you recognise me by any chance?"

"No, sir, I — " the man began, and then his eyes lit up and he exclaimed. "You're the Toff, sir! Mr. Rollison!"

"That's right on the nose," Rollison said. "You know that I'm not half-witted and mean what I say, don't you?"

The man looked puzzled, but was game.

"Yes, sir."

"Well, someone has glued what looks like a bomb on that part of the self-starter, under the bonnet," Rollison said, pointing as he went on: "I have an urgent appointment, and can't handle this job myself. Will you ask your division for help — don't touch it yourself, it's glued on."

"*I* won't touch it!" The policeman straightened up, gulping. "Then — then all of those stories they tell about you *are* true."

"Oh, just one here and there," Rollison said. "I *must* run."

He did run, literally, to the end of the street known as South Canal, and saw three empty taxis pass just before he was near enough to hail, then had to wait several minutes for one, as only buses and private cars passed. His chief purpose in running was to make sure he was not held up by a lot of questions, which would be inevitable if divisional detective officers arrived.

A car slid to a standstill in front of him.

The man with the olive-coloured skin was at the open window, next to the driver, and he said:

"Are you Mr. Rollison?" He pronounced the name Rawlson.

"Yes, but — "

"Can I give you a lift?"

"No," Rollison said, backing away as he went on solemnly: "My mother always told me never to go in cars with strangers." He smiled fleetingly, then espied a taxi with its sign lighted, and he hurried towards it, one hand outstretched.

The man with the American voice *might* shoot him.

But nothing happened, and twenty-five minutes later Rollison got out of the taxi at the corner of Fell Street and, it proved, Rubicon Road. He paid the driver off, then stood at the corner, looking at a house which stood on its own, not really large but certainly not small. On a wooden door were the words: RUBICON HOUSE. No one was in sight when the taxi turned the corner, and Rollison walked slowly and thoughtfully towards the front door.

As he did so, he put one of the blow-pipe cigarettes to his lips.

This street door was unlocked and he went into a square hall, which had a few pieces of heavy furniture and two bamboo chairs, to see a staircase with an arrow on the wall, pointing upwards to Flats 3 and 4. He went up the wide carpeted staircase. As he reached the landing a small, young woman obviously far gone in pregnancy opened the door marked 3, came out and closed the door firmly. He turned towards the other flat across the landing, just saying:

"Good afternoon."

"Good afternoon," the woman returned, and went downstairs with unexpected vigour.

10

Wild, Wild West

ROLLISON STOOD AT THE DOOR of the fourth apartment until he had heard the woman's footsteps clatter down the stairs, patter across the hall, and be cut off by the closing of the street door. Then he turned to the other door and tapped; there was no answer. He banged with the side of his clenched fist but there was still no answer.

He went down on one knee and examined the lock.

It was one of the old fashioned mortice type, difficult to open unless one had the know-how. He had. He took a knife from a special pocket in his trouser waist-band, one with a surprising number of blades — a souvenir of Poland, where knives were knives. This had a pick-lock blade. He used it quickly, not worrying too much about noise as the flat seemed to be empty. The barrel resisted for a long time but at last shot back with a snap of sound greater than he liked.

He paused, but no other sound came.

He pushed the door open cautiously, seeing more and more of the room beyond. Someone *might* be there, lying doggo: Alec George King, for instance. Certainly no one was in this room, which was pleasantly furnished but in no way remarkable.

Two doors led off on one side; one, off the other.

He checked the one first; it was a bathroom. He

checked one of the others to find a small kitchen. So the third door would lead to a bedroom. He pushed it open cautiously, and saw a huge, king size bed, the kind of bed a really tall man could stretch on.

On the bed was a stetson hat, of pale brown leather; and laid out was a suit which, even at first glance, was not a conventional cut. He went farther in, and at the side of the bed saw a pair of western riding boots, not unlike Tommy Loman's. He felt quite certain that the guess that Tommy was to be impersonated was justified. Now, he needed to find out all he could about the plot.

There was a small dressing-table and a chest of drawers; he went through every drawer but found only clothes. A hanging cupboard was filled, half with a man's apparel, half with a woman's; there were no papers. He moved back to the living room and saw a small writing desk, much higher than most; obviously this was to allow Alec George King to get his knees under. The long middle drawer was unlocked and inside were oddments, cheque books, cheque stubs and letters. Rollison scanned the letters which were all demands for payment of overdue bills.

Folded in a bank statement was an even sharper demand for the clearance of an overdraft.

Rollison went through the other papers with extreme care, and found one thing he was looking for in the paying in book. A week ago, King had paid five hundred pounds into his bank account, putting this into credit by over three hundred pounds.

There was nothing to indicate where the money had come from.

Rollison tried two smaller drawers in the bureau; one was unlocked, and contained postage stamps, pins, clips and other trifles. The other was locked. He used the

pick-lock blade of his knife again, and in a few moments
the lock turned and he pulled the drawer open gently.

Inside, were pencilled notes kept in diary form. Obviously the early notes had been jotted down from
memory, for they ran:

Sept. 15/16 — A.W. called.

Sept. 17 — Saw A.W. who outlined the
general idea.

Sept. 17/18 — Talked it over with Effie, who
didn't like it much.

Sept. 19 — Asked A.W. how much it would
be worth — he said £5,000 mini-
mum, £500 at once — cash.

Sept. 20 — Talked it over with Effie again
and she agreed to go ahead if I
would salt the first £500 away.

There followed some notes about a meeting with the
mysterious A.W., his promise to pay a further £500
once King had started 'the job'. There was a cryptic
note: "*I was always good in a Yankee part!*" If that
meant what it seemed to, King did not know the difference between a Yankee and a man from the south west,
but that was a passing thought. How had King started
to earn that second five hundred pounds? There was
another note:

Oct. 3rd — Effie says she can't tell the difference.

Oct. 4th — I did the tape and posted it to A.W.

Oct. 6th — A.W. delighted — he coughed up the
second £500.

Rollison put this aside and looked about the room, saw
a portable record player in one corner and a small tape

recorder with several tapes kept in place with rubber bands, on a nearby stool. One tape was on the recorder, ready to play. Rollison studied the instrument and then switched it on. There were some squeaks and scratches, before a man's voice sounded.

"Sure — that's my name ... I come from Tucson, Arizona ... I work at the Lazy K ranch between Tucson and Nogales ... Well, why not ... Thomas G. Loman ... I am twenty-eight years old ... I was born in Truth and Consequences, New Mexico ... My grandfather was English. He ..."

Rollison heard the tape right through. There was a great deal of repetition, obviously King had been learning all he said by heart, so as to stand in another man's place. Here in the heart of London an Englishman had been learning to take on the identity of Thomas G. Loman! He switched off, thinking that if he took the tape it would warn King that he had been traced; for the time being it would be better to leave it.

Rollison had been here for about half an hour.

The woman whom he assumed to be the Effie of the notes might be back at any moment. There wasn't time to listen to any more tapes. He sat at the desk and scribbled out a copy of the notes and the dates, added the name and address of King's bank manager, and went to the door leading to the landing.

He heard no sound.

He opened the door and stepped on to the landing, turned and bent down to lock the door, always more difficult, with a pick-lock, than opening it. He worried even less about noise, breathed with satisfaction as the lock clicked, straightened up, and turned round.

Framed in the open doorway of Flat 4 was a man who had a stocking drawn over his face, as a mask.

He covered Rollison with an automatic.

.   .   .

Rollison stood utterly still.

So, for a few moments, did the man with the gun.

There were noises from the street; cars, whistling, voices. There was music from the flats below, but up here there was just the stillness and the silence. It seemed a long time before the man in the doorway said:

"So you made it."

"Sooner or later," Rollison replied, "I always do."

"You won't after this," the other said, softly.

"Who knows?" Rollison shrugged.

"I know. You won't live to."

Rollison did not speak, but simply raised his eyebrows. The man in the doorway moved to one side, and said: "Come in."

"I would rather stay here," replied Rollison.

"So I'll have to shoot you there," the masked man retorted.

"I would rather you didn't," said Rollison, and began to walk towards the other.

The man could be the one who had hurled the hand grenade: there was no way of telling. His hand was steady and his voice cold and calculating; there was no way of being sure whether he would shoot. If he, Rollison, allowed himself to go into the other flat, he would be trapped; here, with the stairs and the hallway below, he had some freedom of movement.

He must take a chance and leap for the stairs.

It had to be the right moment — the exact moment.

He was within a yard of the man who could shoot him at point blank range, so it was literally now or never. He actually flexed his muscles to duck and spring towards the stairs when a door opened somewhere below, with a squeak, and footsteps sounded in the hall. The eyes behind the mask swivelled to one side and on that instant Rollison kicked the man on the shin. Gasp of pain and the swivelling of the gun came simultaneously but Rollison had time to chop with the side of his hand on the gun-wrist.

The gun fell.

"Stay down there!" Rollison roared. "Stay there!"

"Effie!" the man cried from behind the mask. "Effie!"

Rollison heard a cry from below, and turned his head to look towards the stairs. It was his first mistake, for the masked man, still gasping, backed into the room and disappeared. The door slammed. Rollison snatched at the handle, but the girl below began to cry out:

"Help, *help*! I'm being robbed."

Rollison stood absolutely still, to try to collect himself.

The man would get away through the window and there was little chance of catching him; if he, Rollison, forced this door and went in he would be breaking and entering, very much on the wrong side of the law.

A man spoke downstairs and the woman whom the masked man had thought was Effie was screaming: he could just distinguish the words:

"Up there, up there!"

Rollison could run down the stairs and out of the house, or more wisely, go down and reason. He had what he wanted. The girl was now alarmed, and the wise thing was to have the police here as soon as possible. He could take them to King's room, and the evidence of the plot to impersonate Tommy Loman would be indisputable.

So he called: "No one's robbing anybody," and he went to the head of the stairs.

The pregnant young woman was standing in the hall, a middle-aged man stood with his arm round her, a scared-looking woman was in the doorway of one of the flats. Effie was sobbing and screaming in a magnificent show of pretended hysterics, and of course she was trading on her condition. She caught sight of him and pointed, screaming even more loudly:

"There he is, there he is!"

Rollison began to walk down the stairs. It was useless attempting to stop the girl, who was undoubtedly trying desperately to give the masked man time to get away. The middle-aged man looked as scared as the woman in the doorway.

"Now, don't upset yourself, my dear, don't upset yourself."

"We — we ought to send for the police," called the middle-aged woman, staring at Rollison defiantly. "That's what I'm going to do."

"I certainly should," urged Rollison, forcing a smile. "I — "

His voice was drowned by the roar of an explosion above their heads. The floor shook, a picture crashed down, the roar went on and pieces of the ceiling fell in, a door banged, then another. There was a split second of uncanny silence followed by a roaring sound.

"Oh, my God!" cried the woman in the doorway.

"He did it, he did it," gasped Effie, still pointing at Rollison. "He's blown the place up!"

Someone had obviously blown the flat up, and the roaring sound was unmistakable; that of fire. Rollison turned and ran upstairs, for the evidence he so badly needed was there, but he saw a red glow at the foot of the door and knew that the Kings' rooms were an inferno. If he opened the door the fire would get out of control so he went back, calling to the man:

"Telephone the police and the fire service. *Hurry!*" He ran through the hall and out of the house, for unless a delayed action bomb had been used the man was still nearby. Rollison raced to the corner, but as he reached it, he saw a motor-cyclist swing out of the rear entrance and roar away, towards the Embankment.

Flames were showing at a window of Rubicon House, people were already in the street, a police siren sounded not far off. Rollison could make himself scarce, or stay and talk; he decided that the sensible course was to stay and talk. That way, he would be less likely to anger the police.

.   .   .

He told part of his story to a divisional detective-sergeant, who telephoned the Division, who telephoned Grice at the Yard, who asked Rollison to go and see him.

"Gladly," Rollison said, the ringing of fire engine bells almost drowning his words. "If one of your chaps can give me a lift. My car — "

"I've heard what happened to your car," said Grice, grimly.

His office was high in the new building at Broadway and Victoria Street, not far from its old site. Rollison had not quite got used to the acres of glass and the similarity of each floor plan. Grice, a tall, spare and angular man with a sallow complexion, was good-looking in a rather severe way. The bridge of his nose was sharp so that the skin at it showed white. On one side of his face was a large, discoloured scar, the aftermath of an explosion which had nearly killed him. At the time he had been opening a box addressed to the Toff. They never referred to that, these days, but it had forged a bond between them which was often strained to breaking point, but never actually snapped.

"Well," Grice said as they shook hands, "it looks as if they mean to get you, Rolly."

"Even I'm beginning to think that," Rollison confessed.

"Did this bomb thrower think you were in the flat?"

"No," Rollison answered. "I think I was an incidental — he wanted to destroy the evidence."

"Oh," said Grice heavily. "What evidence did you find?"

"Notes and tapes which show that a certain actor, Alec George King, has been learning the part of Thomas G. Loman, with a view to impersonating him," answered Rollison. "It was there, Bill."

"How do you know?"

"*Must* I incriminate myself?" demanded Rollison, and Grice smiled faintly:

"Did you actually see it?" he demanded.

"Yes," answered Rollison. "And if I really had to I'd say so in court. The certain thing is that we need to talk to the actor named King and to his wife Effie. Is the fact that their flat was set on fire enough to justify a search for them?"

"We don't need to search for the woman," Grice told him. "I've just had a telephone call from Chelsea. Apparently labour pains started just after you left and she was rushed to Chelsea Hospital to have her baby. There was a rumour that it might be a miscarriage, another that the child was born dead. And in either case a lot of people are going to say that it was your visit to her home which really brought things on."

II

Whitemail

AFTER A LONG PAUSE, Rollison said: "That's what they're going to say, are they Bill?"

"You know perfectly well that they are."

"Some of them may but you know as well as I do that most of them won't," Rollison said with forced lightness.

"Was the house destroyed?"

"The upper part was gutted, and the downstairs flats are uninhabitable."

"Are your chaps searching the wreckage?"

"The place is still burning."

"One tape from a bundle in the front room would be enough to prove my point," Rollison said.

"There isn't likely to be even the remains of a tape," Grice told him. "They say the upper part went up in no time, and the roof has fallen in."

"Is there a call out for King?"

"To come and see his wife at the hospital, yes. Rolly, we've nothing on King, and you know it."

"Bill," said Rollison, "these people are killers. I think King's life is in grave danger because he could tell us — all right, you — what's been going on. If I were you I wouldn't simply try to find him to soothe his wife down, I'd try to find him because his life is in acute danger.

There's nothing in the world to stop you from putting out a general call."

Slowly, Grice, conceded: "He could be in danger, I suppose. I'll have a general call put out for him." He lifted one of three receivers on his desk, and gave instructions, put down the telephone and went on to Rollison almost in the same breath. "The description of the motor-cyclist who attacked you and this motor-cyclist is identical. Green helmet, black goggles, on the big side, and splay-footed."

"Any trace of him?" asked Rollison hopefully.

"I'll tell you the moment there is," Grice promised.

"Thanks. What more do you want from me now?"

"A statement covering why you went to Rubicon House and what you did and anything you can say to help us find the motor-cyclist."

"That will be a pleasure,' 'Rollison replied with relish.

Half an hour later, he was taken downstairs to the garage beneath the new building, and the first thing he saw in a bay near the ramp was his Bristol. A police mechanic moved over towards him and a sergeant whom Grice had sent down with him.

"Did you get that bomb off?" asked Rollison.

"No, sir, I did not!" the mechanic replied. "We sent for a bomb disposal squad, and they came pronto and prised it off. They said it would have blown up half the car, and you with it. It's all okay now, though, sir."

"Yes," said Rollison. "Thanks very much."

All right, he kept repeating to himself. *All right.* One moment he could have laughed at the ludicrousness of the fact that so much had happened. He must have been recognised by Effie, who had sent for the motor-cyclist: what other explanation could there be. At least, he wasn't being held. He got into the car and saw that it was a quarter past five.

Pamela Brown was due at half past six, and — Good Lord! He'd forgotten Jack Fisher!

What would he find when he reached his flat?

Outside were policemen and near them roughly-dressed men, Ebbutt's men, who had come to keep an eye on him at Jolly's request.

He found Tommy Loman talking earnestly to Jack Fisher, in the big room, glasses in hand, whisky and a syphon of soda on a low table between them. He crept in the side way on recognising Tommy's voice. He gave a soft whistle at the kitchen door, to alert Jolly, who turned at once.

"Are you all right, sir?"

"Yes. Why shouldn't I be?"

"The radio mentioned you in connection with a fire in Chelsea, sir."

"Did they mention Tommy Loman?"

"No, sir — no names were mentioned except that of a Mrs. King — "

"Jolly," interrupted Rollison, "even our Grice tried to whitemail me about Effie King. In fact I still owe him a comment on what I think of her." He leaned against the sink. "How long has Fisher been here?"

"About twenty minutes, sir. I thought it best to give them a drink and let them find their own level. It has been rather amusing — they are vying with each other in their knowledge of you!"

"*What?*" breathed Rollison.

"It is true, sir. Fisher has obviously followed your activities for many years with close interest, and whilst here Mr. Loman has learned a great deal from the press cuttings books and case histories. Will Mr. Fisher stay to dinner?"

"No," answered Rollison. "I'd like him to go before Miss Brown arrives. Has anyone called?"

"No, sir. Mr. Ebbutt has sent six men who have stationed themselves in the street and at the back of the building. Two policemen are back and front, too. I don't think there is too much danger," Jolly added, soothingly.

"I shouldn't be too sure," said Rollison.

"Seriously, sir?"

"A man who escaped on a motor-cycle lobbed another bomb, this time a fire-bomb, at the house I was in at Chelsea," said Rollison. "Then he seems to have escaped through a window and leapt on his motor-cycle as Loman would leap on his trusty steed. I'll give you all details later. Er — Jolly."

"Sir?"

"Miss Pamela Brown carries a pistol."

"Indeed, sir."

"Yes, indeed. If you think there is any need, take the gun out of her bag, take the bullets out, and put the gun back."

"I will certainly do my best, sir. Have you any reason to believe that Mr. Fisher is armed?"

"I don't yet know what to make of Mr. Fisher," Rollison replied thoughtfully. "I shall soon find out." He went to the study-cum-living room, to hear Fisher say with both heat and emphasis:

"I still say that his most remarkable case was the one about the voodoo doll. Did you read that?"

"Why, sure thing, I read all about it," answered Loman. "It was fascinating, Jack. But the story I prefer is the one when he was helping those fallen women — "

"Angels."

"Huh?"

"Fallen angels."

"Sure, that's what he called them," conceded Loman, "but — "

"Good evening, gentlemen," Rollison strode forward

into the room at a pace suggesting that he couldn't get in fast enough and had heard nothing of what had been said. "Mr. Fisher, I can't say how sorry I am that I'm late."

"It's perfectly all right, Mr. Rollison. Don't worry at all."

"Jolly's got you a drink, I see?... How about another?" He refilled Fisher's glass while the man stared at him as if not quite sure that he was real. Soon, he was drinking their health, they were asking questions about the past and the future, but neither mentioned the present until Fisher asked:

"Did they find that motor-cyclist?"

"They haven't yet," answered Rollison.

"But he's the key to the whole thing!" cried Fisher. "Once they know why he tried to kill you the rest is bound to fall into place. Isn't it, Mr. Rollison?" He spun round to Rollison for confirmation. "They mustn't let him get away!"

"They'll catch him, sooner or later," Rollison said reassuringly.

"They should have caught him already," Fisher declared angrily. "I — " He broke off, and forced a smile. "Well, I don't want to spoil a wonderful evening like this by losing my temper, do I?"

"Lost tempers can do a world of good," Rollison soothed. "I came nearer to losing mine this evening than I have for a long, long time."

"You!" exclaimed Fisher.

"How?" inquired Loman.

"You can't start a story like that and not tell us what happened," protested Fisher.

"No, I suppose I can't," Rollison said. "Well, it was something like this." He moved to his desk and touched a switch which meant that in the kitchen Jolly would hear what he was saying. "I came upon the motor-cyclist again, or he came upon me," he went on. "He was in the home — the flat — of an actor who plays character parts, and whose wife is going to have a baby."

He paused.

Both men stared, and he was sure that Jolly was suddenly spellbound, pausing in the middle of whatever culinary art he was engaged upon. Very carefully, he went on:

"The motor-cyclist first wrecked the place, with a hand-grenade I suspect, and finished it off with a fire-bomb. All of us were lucky to escape with our lives."

"*All* of you?" asked Loman, faintly.

"Did the motor-cyclist get away again?" demanded Fisher.

"He did."

"No wonder you were mad!"

"I wasn't exactly angry about that, I was too glad to be alive," Rollison retorted. "But I began to lose my temper when someone suggested that I'd thrown the bomb — "

"Who on earth accused you of *that*?" cried Fisher.

"The little mother-to-be," stated Rollison.

"The little *bitch*!" Fisher's voice rose. "As if you — "

His championship of Rollison was almost too much to stand, Rollison thought; and wondered whether Fisher got all his thrills vicariously.

"Would you say that?" asked Loman, quietly. He had been eyeing Rollison very thoughtfully all the time. "In that condition women can say some wild things." When neither of the others commented he added lamely: "I guess."

"Women are always saying wild things," grumbled Fisher.

"Richard," asked Loman. "What made you angry?"

"They began to blame me when the woman had to be hurried off to hospital," Rollison stated carefully.

Fisher groaned: "Oh, no." He backed a pace to a chair and sat on the arm, gaping at Rollison, while Loman simply took another sip of his drink and remarked:

"They had to blame someone. Did the woman see the man or the motor-cycle?"

"Not as far as I know."

"Well, perhaps they didn't believe in him," said Loman, with a slow smile. "Perhaps they were ready to believe that the man who won all these trophies was capable of anything." There was a hint of laughter in his eyes. "Now if they started to suggest the baby was yours — "

"How on earth could they?" demanded Fisher, angrily.

The problem, thought Rollison, was going to be to get the over-earnest Fisher away before Pamela Brown arrived, and while he was dwelling on that the telephone bell rang. He sat at his desk and pulled the telephone towards him while Loman went to the far end of the Trophy Wall, and Fisher glanced at his watch.

"This is Richard Rollison," Rollison announced.

"This is Stevens of the *Daily Globe*," a man replied. "Good evening, Mr. Rollison. Were you at the scene of a fire in Fell Street, Chelsea, this afternoon?"

"Yes," answered Rollison.

"Did you raise the alarm, Mr. Rollison?"

"No. I was too busy chasing the man who had started the fire."

"Did you catch him, sir?"

"No. He escaped on a motor-cycle."

"Do you *know* he was the man who started the fire?" asked the reporter, with mild insistence.

"I am satisfied he did but I couldn't prove it."

"I see, sir. Were you in or outside the house at the time?"

"Inside."

"Thank you very much, Mr. Rollison. I have a statement from a Mr. Hindle, who lived in one of the flats downstairs, to the effect that you appear to have been upstairs just before the explosion which preceded the fire."

"I was," stated Rollison.

"And according to this gentleman, sir, the wife of the tenant of the flat upstairs believed you had been in her flat during her absence. Had you sir?"

"If she was absent, how could she know?"

"Isn't that evading the question, sir?"

Rollison found himself teetering between annoyance and amusement; and for the moment amusement won. He chuckled.

"No comment," he said.

"Mr. Rollison, in the public interest — "

"In the public interest and in the interest of the *Globe* newspaper, no comment," insisted Rollison.

"Mr. Rollison — your duty is surely — "

"Do you know, Mr. Stevens, I have known many police officers less naive in their questions and far less likely to prejudge an issue than you." Rollison said. "No more questions — at least, no more answers." Now, he was neither amused nor annoyed, but very wary.

"Mr. Rollison," the newspaperman went on. "I don't know that you are in a position to flaunt the Press. The lady in question, the wife of an actor, gave birth to a male child, this afternoon, a premature birth believed to be as a result of the incident. It is of considerable importance in your own as well as the public interest, for the truth to be known. Before going to hospital she accused you of forcing entry into her flat, and leaving behind a high explosive bomb which wrecked not only the flat but led to the destruction of the upper part of the house. In the public interest — "

"Mr. Stevens," Rollison interrupted.

"Yes, sir."

"Do I understand you want a statement from me?"

"Yes, sir. In the public — "

"The woman is a liar," Rollison said.

"Mr. Rollison! A woman in such a condition would hardly make such wild accusations without some reason to believe them. If you were in her flat, sir, she may well have reason to believe you did cause the destruction — "

"I did not," Rollison said, "and her condition might well have made her hysterical."

"*Were* you in her flat?" demanded the newspaperman, in his persistent way. "That is the crucial question. If you can deny that, the *Globe* will naturally publish the denial. If on the other hand you cannot or will not deny it, then the *Globe* will of course publish the lady's statement — "

"And lay itself wide open for action for libel," Rollison interrupted. "Let me ask *you* a question, Mr. Stevens. Have you interviewed the husband, Alec King?"

"No, sir."

"Why not?"

"We have not been able to trace him, but the moment we do — "

"Now that really will be in the public interest," said Rollison, firmly. "Find the missing husband, and you might find the answers to most of the questions you've asked and a lot you haven't asked. Goodnight."

On that crisply uttered word, he rang off.

12

Pamela Brown

ROLLISON TURNED FROM the telephone to find both of his visitors watching him, Jack Fisher frowning, Tommy Loman with characteristic calmness; he seemed always to be looking not only at but beyond the Toff, like a man used to peering into long distances.

"Was a newspaper trying to blackmail you?" demanded Fisher.

"More like whitemail," answered Rollison lightly. "Even the police are not above trying it at times. Forget that, please. How about another drink?"

"No, really, I must go," said Fisher, as if regretfully. "I have an appointment at half-past six." He gave a smile which brightened his blue eyes. "A date, you know."

"You want to be careful," remarked Loman. "You don't want to give anyone an excuse for whitemailing you. Does he, Richard?"

Fisher frowned, until suddenly he saw the point and gave a hearty laugh, while Rollison chuckled and Loman regarded him with almost benign approval. Fisher left, effusive in his thanks, and Rollison sent him on his way with a quiet:

"How could I do less for a man who was such a help?"

Fisher, apparently covered in embarrassment, hurried down the stairs. Rollison turned back into the big room, to find Tommy Loman regarding him with his eyes smiling but his face set and even stern. Rollison was strangely aware of the contrast; it was seldom that he had to look upwards at a man, or be looked down upon. They stood for a few moments and to Rollison this seemed the first quiet spell he had known all day.

At last, Loman sank into a large armchair, diagonally across a corner, and Rollison sat in a rather smaller chair, opposite.

"Is that right — he did you a service?" asked Loman thoughtfully.

"Yes."

"He's a funny little guy."

"How funny?" asked Rollison.

"Cute." Then Loman went on: "Kind of nervous. Didn't you think he was nervous?"

"I make some people nervous," Rollison remarked.

"Not that kind of nervous," replied Loman. "He was surprised to see me here when he arrived, *I* seemed to make him kind of jumpy." That slow, attractive smile dawned and stayed.

"Have you ever looked up at a giraffe without expecting to?" asked Rollison lightly. "Tommy, I've a guest coming for dinner and I'd like to talk to her alone for half an hour or so before we eat. Would you mind —?"

"I can take a bath," Loman interrupted, instantly placing his hands on the arms of his chair. "You don't have to eat with me, Richard. I can go into the kitchen with Mr. Jolly, he — "

"I only need half-an-hour tête-à-tête," Rollison said firmly. "I — " There was a ring at the front door, and he broke off to say: "This may be her."

Loman was on his feet in a trice, uncoiling like a giant spring. He went to the spare room along one passage while Jolly went to the front door along the other.

Rollison could see the lounge-hall from here but before he saw the visitor he knew it was Pamela Brown, because she said in an eager voice:

"Mr. Rollison is expecting me."

"Miss Brown?" asked Jolly, standing aside.

"That's right — Pamela Brown."

"Mr. Rollison is certainly expecting you," Jolly said, and turned as Pamela entered.

My! thought Rollison.

She looked ravishing in a dark green dress with a deep V neckline, her hair piled high, her eyes bright, ear-rings dangling and a brooch glittering at her bosom. The dress rustled faintly as she walked. It fell just above her knees, and for the first time Rollison saw that she had beautiful legs; he already knew that she moved with youthful grace. He was out of his chair and on his feet when she came in with one arm held out; he extended both hands and took hers.

"Ravishing!" he uttered the word that had first come to mind.

"Oh, *thank* you!" She had nice, cool hands, and she looked into his eyes, not about the room. "It's lovely to be here."

He held on to her hands a moment longer than was necessary, then drew her into the room. She looked about her, at and beyond the Trophy Wall, at the paintings on one other wall, at a group of four etchings of old London, and at the pieces of antique furniture ranging from Elizabethan through Georgian and Regency to Victorian all of which fitted perfectly in their places and merged together.

"What will you have to drink?" he asked.

"May I have something soft — ginger ale or bitter lemon?"

"Of course," he said.

"You see," she exclaimed with the familiar naivete. "I don't drink alcohol."

"Not at *all*?" He was surprised.

"Never." She gave the word a slight emphasis and her eyes danced. "What a *lovely* flat you have. And — may I have a closer look at those macabre things on the wall?" She took her drink and they moved towards the wall as she went on almost in the same breath. "Did I see Baby Blue Eyes in the street as I was parking my car?"

"He'd just been in for a drink," said Rollison. "How well do you know him?"

She looked at him quite sharply. "I'd never met him until this morning," she said. "What makes you think I know him?"

"He didn't mention you to the police," said Rollison drily. "I couldn't believe that was an accident."

"Oh, poof! He was dazzled by the Toff and just didn't see me!"

"Any man who doesn't notice you is no man," replied Rollison.

"But how *gallant*!" Her eyes danced again. "Well, let's say he was so overcome when he realised who you were and what had happened, that he forgot me."

"Which would make him even less of a man."

"You *are* determined to live up to your reputation!" She looked away from him at the silk stocking which was draped over a polished brass bracket, and asked with new-found solemnity: "*Is* that a murder weapon?"

"Yes. Did you know about this wall and my reputation or had you been looking me up?" he asked.

"Who could tell me?" she asked.

"Any newspaperman who wanted to."

"Oh," she said. "Yes, I suppose so. Well, as a matter of fact, I knew."

"Just as you knew I was going to meet Tommy Loman at the airport."

"Yes," she said. How beautifully her eyes glowed. "Mr. Rollison — "

"Richard."

"Richard, I cannot tell a lie!" She was acting very slightly, as if this in many ways amused her; she was laughing partly at herself, partly at the situation, partly at him. She lowered her voice and went on melodramatically: "I am a private inquiry agent."

"Good God!" he gasped.

"You mean I fooled you?" She was delighted.

"You fooled me utterly. At the very least I thought you were a seductress, plotting to seduce Tommy Loman."

"Oh, nothing so unexciting," she replied. "*He* isn't the man I would try to seduce! I wrote to Tommy Loman and invited him in your name to come to London and see you," she went on simply. "I signed the letter P. Brown, for Richard Rollison."

This time Rollison was really astounded, but all he said was: "In *my* name?"

"Yes. I thought he would come if you invited him, whereas if a strange woman wrote, he might shrug it off. Aren't you going to ask why?"

"Yes," Rollison said heavily. "Why?"

"Because I believed he would run into trouble if he just arrived here and had nowhere to go for help."

"I see," said Rollison.

He was studying this young woman much more closely, reasonably sure that she was telling the truth but fully aware of how easy it would be to be fooled — 'seduced'! — into accepting her on her face value. The harder he looked, the more flawless her complexion and the more beautiful her eyes; and the dress was most enticing, showing just enough of her white bosom and shoulders. She seemed to sense that it was a moment for silence and she made no attempt to speak or prompt him.

"Why should he run into trouble?" he asked.

"Because he was coming to claim a fortune which someone else wants to take from him."

"What fortune?"

"A great-uncle, his grandfather's brother, left a fortune and Thomas G. Loman is the only legatee," she said. "And someone thought it a good idea to stand-in for the real Loman and collect the inheritance."

"How did you know that?" Rollison asked quietly.

For the first time, she hesitated, and he preferred that she should; the series of swift answers made her sound almost glib. She sipped her ginger ale, swallowing slowly as if her mouth was dry, and finally went on:

"It's a very long story, Mr. Rollison. If I'd been able to produce facts and evidence I think I would have gone to the police and told them — after all, it's really their job, isn't it? But I had only an old man's fears and suspicions to go on, and — and a feeling, an intuition. *Please* don't laugh."

"I wouldn't laugh even at a man's intuition," Rollison assured her.

"You see, old Josh — that's the great-uncle — had a kind of persecution mania. He was ninety-one, and remarkably fit physically and no slouch mentally, except in this one way — he thought someone was always trying to rob him, and had a fear that someone outside the family would get his money when he died."

"When *did* he die?"

"Just a month ago."

"A natural death?"

"Yes — indisputably, I think."

"Was there an autopsy?"

"Yes — I work with my father and a brother, Mr.
Rol — "

"Richard."

"Thank you, Richard! And my father has been in the
profession for a long time. The police respect him and
he telephoned the Superintendent of the Hampstead
Division where Mr. Clayhanger lived, and said an
autopsy might be advisable although a death certificate
was signed. One was carried out by Kenneth Soames,
and you must know pathologists don't come any
better."

"I do," admitted Rollison, becoming more and more
intrigued. "What was the cause of death?"

"Cerebral haemorrhage. The old man had had two
mild strokes so that wasn't surprising."

"And can't easily be induced," Rollison remarked.
"Did he have a nurse?"

"Yes — a day and a night nurse in his last months.
He — " She leaned forward and touched Rollison's hand
with her cool fingers before going on: "My father went
to see him first, and took his fears seriously because he
had such a lucid mind. He knew there was a nephew in
Arizona, who was the only surviving relative, and wanted
him traced *and* wanted to make sure he got the inheritance. Then one day my father was ill and my brother
away and I had to go and see old Josh." She gave a
funny little strangled laugh. "You'll never believe it, but
he took a great liking to me."

"I will try to make myself believe it," Rollison said
drily.

"And I've never met a man I liked more, whatever his
age," Pamela Brown went on. "So after that I would
take the weekly report now and again; saying that we
hadn't yet traced Thomas George Loman, and found
nothing to suggest anyone else had any claim to the

inheritance. All he ever said was: 'You will keep trying, won't you'."

"Did you ever find the slightest cause for his fear that there would be a false claimant?" asked Rollison.

"No," answered Pamela. "No, we didn't. We found one or two other distant relatives who had no expectations from his will and checked them carefully: there didn't seem the slightest danger from them, except, possibly, one elderly — or rather middle-aged man. But what we did do was trace Thomas G. Loman."

"*You* traced him?" exclaimed Rollison.

"Yes," she assured him. "We hadn't much to go on. His mother had left England as a young child and not kept in touch with her father, but we sent her name round to all the detective agencies in the south west —"

"Why the south west?"

"Oh, I'm sorry. It was known that she'd married a rancher somewhere in Texas. Anyhow, Richard, we traced the name — Clayhanger isn't so common — in the records of an old Methodist church in Lubbock, Texas, and then discovered they'd moved from there to Austin and later to New Mexico. I *can* show you the reports from America showing how Tommy was traced. We've a kind of family tree showing name changes and marriages and two divorces — until finally we discovered Thomas G. Loman, whose mother was the daughter of a Mr. and Mrs. Josh Clayhanger. All the rest of the family died out but for two distant cousins by marriage, and Tommy G., who still worked as a cowboy but didn't own his own spread. That means — "

"I know what a 'spread' is," Rollison assured her.

"I'm sorry. Well — there he was, the only legatee, who would inherit over a million pounds," said Pamela Brown, simply. "We would just have sent for him, had someone not stolen the reports from America and our final report to old Josh. That was why we involved you. We felt there *was* something very odd going on, and by bringing you in this way, you would be intrigued. We hadn't expected such quick action. Thank goodness Josh knew we'd traced Tommy, and — " Pamela broke off and stood up and moved about the room, then stood with her back to the Trophy Wall, facing Rollison. Her face was set, her eyes lacked fire but held their brilliance. "When we told the old man he said: 'Thank God. You make sure nothing happens to him. Do you hear? You make sure nothing happens to him'!" Pamela paused and her eyes were misty as if the recollection brought tears very close to the surface. Slowly, she went on: "He was so sure someone would try to get Tommy's money, it was almost uncanny. As if," she went on, looking defiantly at Rollison, "as if he had second sight."

"Perhaps he did," said Rollison gently.

"*You* think it's possible."

"Any man who doesn't believe in second sight hasn't been about much," Rollison answered. "Yes. I think it's possible."

"Well," went on Pamela, relaxing and going back to her chair, hoisting and smoothing her dress as she sat down, "we felt we had to try something. The police wouldn't take any notice of such a story — or at least they wouldn't be likely to take any action — so we thought of you. We wrote to Tommy G., as I've explained, and told him it was extremely important that he should come straight to you. We meant to be there when he arrived." She gave her most charming smile. "You would hardly have refused to help, would you?"

"The devious way is too often wrong," Rollison said drily. "After a story like this, though, I would have helped on a straight request. Why didn't you come to see me first?"

Again Pamela leaned towards him and touched his hand, this time pleading with him to believe her. It was some time before she went on, in a husky voice:

"We were going to, but the whole family went down with two-day 'flu. I went first and recovered first, the others are still not over it. And I'd had a cable from Tommy saying when he would be here only on the morning of his arrival. I did the only thing that seemed sensible, let events speak for themselves. And you must admit they did," she finished, with mingled triumph and defiance. "Mr. Rollison — Richard — that's everything I can tell you. I didn't dream they would try to kill us in the car, I don't know whether I showed it but I've never been so frightened. Have you?" she asked, in a low-pitched voice.

"I don't know whether Richard has," said Tommy G. Loman, striding in from the door leading to the spare room and Jolly's quarters. "I've never been so frightened as I am now. No, sir, that's the simple truth."

He stood looking down from his great height at Rollison; it was a long time before he turned towards the girl.

13

"Never So Frightened"

VERY SLOWLY, Tommy's expression changed.

He had been listening for a long time, of course; anything else would be beyond the average man's endurance. Certainly he had heard enough to make him put his heart into his voice, and the way he looked at Rollison seemed to ask: "And what are you going to do about it?" Only slowly had he realised how attractive the girl was, and as that grew on him his mouth dropped open and his eyes became huge.

"Good evening," Pamela said in a small voice. "I am Pamela Brown."

Tommy gulped; and only when he gulped did his Adam's apple reveal its prominence. He gulped twice.

"Jumping cats," he said, breathlessly. *"You're* the one who wrote to me?"

"Yes."

"You signed that letter P. Brown."

"I *am* P. Brown."

"Great galloping gophers," breathed Tommy. "Why, you're beautiful."

She did not simper, play coy, or otherwise use the coquettish kind of feminine wile, but said simply:

"Thank you."

"You most surely are."

"Thank you."

"And still frightened?" inquired Rollison mildly.

"Yes," she answered quietly.

"Miss Pamela," said Tommy in a weak voice. "You sure made me forget how scared I was."

For the first time since his appearance, a hint of merriment showed in Pamela's eyes, and she replied:

"You almost did the same for me."

"I did?" Tommy looked delighted.

"Yes," she went on, demurely. "Every moment I expect you to bang your head against the ceiling."

"My head," he echoed, and glanced up. "No, ma'am, that ceiling's all of eight feet. I couldn't bang my head against it even if I jumped. Pink-eared jack-rabbits, I didn't think young women like you grew in England."

"England is a remarkable place," replied Pamela.

"Yes, ma'am. And it sure is green." Tommy looked round and found a chair, lowered himself into it and for comfort's sake had to stretch his legs straight out. Now they were all at equal eye-level, and the strain of craning necks had gone. "Miss Brown," he went on, "that was a mighty strange story you just told."

"Yes, I suppose so," Pamela agreed. "But true."

"I'll strike the first man who calls you a liar, ma'am."

"Not many people do," said Pamela, and she finished her ginger ale.

As Rollison got up to refill her glass and pour a drink for Tommy, he noticed two things. Tommy was staring at Pamela Brown as if he could not tear his gaze away from her, and Jolly appeared in the doorway. This was Jolly's way of announcing that dinner would be ready in ten minutes; if Rollison wanted it delayed he must now say so or for this occasion hold his peace. Rollison nodded, Jolly disappeared, Rollison joined the others with the drinks.

"Scotch on the rocks," he said to Tommy.

"That's just right," Tommy said appreciatively. He raised his glass to them both, sipped, and had hardly swallowed before he went on: "Richard, I'm not so sure you're right about my life being in danger. Yours is, I guess, and Miss Pamela's, because you know too much."

"And now you know too much," Rollison pointed out.

"Do these other folk know that?"

"They know you're here," Rollison said. "They know all that matters." He stood with his back to the fireplace and looked at them both, and told them what he had found and what had happened at Rubicon House, but he did not use the name Rubicon, just said 'a house in Chelsea'. They sat, spellbound, until he had finished by telling them what the man from the *Globe* had said. It seemed a long time before Tommy G. remarked quietly:

"So they've been training a guy to impersonate me."

"Yes." Rollison was brisk.

"And now he's missing."

"Yes. But no one's yet tried very hard to find him," Rollison replied. "The odds are that he will stay in hiding until he thinks he sees an opportunity to take your place, or because he's afraid that now the truth is suspected, the people who hired him might decide they ought to stop. Once caught by the police, he would be pretty strong evidence of the impersonation story, and would probably talk easily. Until he's caught, there can't be any proof." When neither of the others responded to this, Rollison went on slowly: "At the moment there is only one person who could be made to talk."

"The motor-cyclist!" exclaimed Pamela.

"We don't know where he is and can't talk to him," Rollison pointed out. "No: King's wife, Effie. And I suspect that the attempt to throw suspicion on me at her

house was to make sure I couldn't go after the motor-
cyclist. The arrival of her baby means that neither I
nor the police can push her too hard, although from what
I saw of her size, the birth wasn't very premature, and
she's getting all the sympathy she can. Trying to get in
to see her would be worse than breaking into an armed
camp. Everyone in the hospital will be guarding the poor
little mother, and — "

"Richard," interrupted Pamela.

"Yes?"

"Could this place which was damaged possibly be
Rubicon House?"

Rollison said sharply: "Yes. Does it mean anything
to you?"

"It's the house where the other relative of old Josh
lives," said Pamela, slowly. "The one whom I didn't trust
at all. He is a Mr. Hindle, at Flat 1, Rubicon House."

"About five-eight, plump, grey-haired, a bald patch,
a broad nose, slightly tip-tilted, a round chin, rather a
vague man to look at?"

"That's him exactly!" cried Pamela.

"He's the man who was so eager to help and believe
Effie King," declared Rollison. "Well, well, well! What
a remarkable coincidence that they are living in the same
house!"

"He owns the house — that is, Mr. Hindle does, and
lets off three flats. The rents are almost his only income."

For a moment there was utter silence.

Jolly broke it from the raised alcove by saying:
"Dinner is served, sir."

.   .   .

Rollison needed time to ponder.

The discovery excited Pamela but her excitement soon
faded and she sat looking down at her plate or looking up

and catching Tommy's eyes. He seemed never to look anywhere else. Jolly served first a halved grapefruit steeped in sherry and covered with sugar and heated under the grill, then a morsel of lemon sole with a sauce which melted in the mouth, finally saddle of lamb with peas and new potatoes which made believe it was spring. Half-way through the main course, they began to talk, slowly at first and then with more animation, until finally Pamela said:

"Richard, you must tell the police about Hindle. They must look for him as well as for King."

"Yes," Rollison agreed. "I'm trying to see all the angles." He finished his lamb, and went to the hotplate by the side of the table. "More for either of you?" Tommy's eyes lit up, and he carved from the saddle of lamb hidden until then under a silver cover, adding peas and potatoes. "Pamela?"

"I shouldn't really."

"Keep Tommy company," urged Rollison, and added: "I'll go and talk to the Yard and to one or two friends of mine — I'll be back before Jolly brings in the dessert." He went to the kitchen where Jolly was whipping cream for a sherry trifle, and said: "Hold it until I'm through, Jolly, I won't be long."

"This won't spoil, sir."

"Good!" Rollison hurried out by the fire-escape, which was reached through the kitchen door. There was still light enough to see two men on duty in the courtyard behind the house, bounded on one side by these old Gresham Terrace houses, on one by a row of mews all three hundred years old and more, on two sides by big new buildings of ferro-concrete. He had a word with the two policemen and also with a third man, small and wiry, who had been sent here by Bill Ebbutt, after Jolly and Ebbutt his oldest and staunchest friend.

"Hallo, Percy."

"Anything for us to *do*, Mr Ar?"

"Just look after me," Rollison quipped.

"That'll be the day," replied Percy Wrighton, at one time a light-weight boxer near the top of his class. "There's a pack of reporters out the front. Don't say I didn't warn you."

"I'll never say a word against you," promised Rollison, and went through an alleyway into the mews and then round the corner into Gresham Terrace.

At least thirty men were there, with a sprinkling of women. He saw several with cameras, and also saw a camera on a tripod in the porch of a house opposite number 25, covering his front door. A cackle of voices sounded, surprisingly loud in the street. Two policemen were keeping the crowd away on one side so as to allow traffic to pass, other plainclothes men were on duty. On the fringes of the crowd were more of Bill Ebbutt's men from the East End.

Parked some distance along but this side of the crowd was Ebbutt's Model T Ford, his most prized possession. Rollison guessed that Ebbutt was sitting at the wheel of this, and walked up and stood alongside. There was Ebbutt, a mountain of a man, paunch squeezed against the steering wheel, his breath wheezing. The car was close to an empty house with 'For Sale' posters in the windows.

"Bill," whispered Rollison. "Move over."

"Who—?" began Ebbutt, turning his head swiftly; then he gasped. "Mr. Ar!" He eased his bulk to one side, and Rollison climbed up. "They're after you tonight, Mr. Ar. Anyone would think no one had ever had a baby before."

"Just a human story, you know how they love the

angle," Rollison said lightly. "May I use the running board to make a speech from? It won't take long."

"You going to *talk* to them lousy newshounds?" demanded Ebbutt.

"They're not lousy, Bill — just story conscious. May I?"

"Use the roof if it will help," Ebbutt replied.

"Thanks. I'd like you to go round to the police and your chaps and tell them to watch all the people on the fringe of the crowd. It's just possible one of them has a hand grenade."

"Strewth," wheezed Ebbutt.

"I'll stand on the running board and you give a toot or two on the horn," said Rollison. The rubber bulb of an old fashioned horn was close to Ebbutt's hand, and it was said that he could get a dozen different notes out of this. Rollison got out and rounded the car and climbed on the running board. As soon as he was holding on to the door, Ebbutt punched and poked at the horn, making an unmistakable tune.

"*Da-di-di-da-di-daa-da! Da-di-di-da-di-da!*"

Rollison found himself singing to the second rendering:

"Come to the cookhouse door, boys; come to the cookhouse door."

The men and women in the crowd swung round and a man shouted: "There's Rollison!" Another called: "There's the Toff!" Others called out, many ran and cameras flashed. Ebbutt slid out of the driver's seat on his errand. Soon questions were being flung at Rollison.

"Were you at Rubicon House?"

"Did you know she was going to have a baby?"

"Had you ever seen her before?"

"Was it an attempt to kill you, Toff?"

"Have you seen her since the baby was born?"

"*Bill!*" called Rollison in a tone which could be heard by nearly everyone present, "give one long blast on your horn, will you?"

"Glad to," Ebbutt said, and immediately the horn hooted a hoarse, low-pitched sound which cut across the questions, silencing everybody. Then it wailed into silence itself, and Rollison raised his voice:

"I've no time to answer questions but I'll make a statement. Ready?" After a chorus of 'we're ready' and 'fire away', he went on: "I went to Rubicon House to look for a character actor named Alec George King, who lives there. I did not know him or his wife, Effie. King wasn't there and I believe he's in acute danger — of losing his life. Every newspaper must have a picture of him somewhere in its files. I don't give a damn what you say about me provided you make everyone realise I want to see this man — urgently."

"What do the police say?" a man called out.

"They can't act on this, yet."

"Do you think King started the fire?" a man demanded.

"Did *you* start the fire?" another called.

"No, to both," Rollison said. "The man or woman who started the fire was medium size, and King is six feet seven. The man or woman rode a motor-cycle, and wore a stocking mask. I can't tell you anything about the man who started the fire but I can tell you about Alec George King." He paused for a moment and then called: "Is there anyone here from the *Globe*?"

"Yes — I am!" a tall, fair-haired man showed clearly in the street lamplight.

"Is your name Stevens?"

"No — we've no one named Stevens on the paper."

"Check at your office for me, will you?" asked Rollison. "A man purporting to be from the *Globe* — "

"Mr. Ar!" bellowed Ebbutt, fear overcoming the hoarseness of his voice, "look out!"

A policeman shouted: "He's throwing a bomb!"

Rollison saw the crowd freeze, momentarily, except for two policemen and a man on the pavement, whose right hand was raised in the act of throwing. For an awful moment it seemed as if most of those present were mesmerised by fear, but suddenly there was a wave of movement from the car; the crowd seemed to billow and sway rather than turn and run.

In the half-light, Rollison could see the dark spheroid in the air, curving an arc towards him and the Model T. He dared not take his eyes off it; dared not look to see if the man had turned and run once he had hurled the bomb. Rollison felt sure it would be a hand grenade, which would explode on contact with car or road. He had never been nearer to death. He stepped down from the running board and cupped his hands, fully aware that if he caught the grenade it might blow up in his hands.

He caught it.

It did not go off instantly.

With great deliberation he drew back his arm and threw the grenade towards the empty house; and he had never been nearer praying. No one was close to the spot, but if it exploded outside it could do unspeakable harm.

It crashed through the window.

A split-second later, it exploded.

14

Capture

ROLLISON WAS AWARE only of one thing: the flash of
the explosion and the strange shape of the star-like hole
which appeared in the window. He threw himself down,
covering his head with his arms, and heard the roar and
felt the blast. He was lifted bodily, but only a few inches.
He heard the thudding and cracking of glass, mortar,
pieces of brick and wood which fell into the street; one
fell, lightly, on the small of his back; another, sharper,
hit the fingers of his right hand.

The sounds all merged into one; a kind of roaring.

He only knew that the bomb had not exploded among
people, among the reporters, that it had caused as little
damage as possible; that he was alive.

He was oblivious of everything else; of the man who
had thrown the bomb, for instance. And what happened
in Gresham Terrace on that long-to-be-remembered
night was seen by different people in different little sil-
houettes; none saw everything, but the picture of all that
had happened was formed when every segment was put
together.

.   .   .

Jolly at one window, Pamela Brown and Tommy G.
Loman from another, saw a foreshortened view. The

sudden shouting had drawn them to the windows and Loman had been the first to fling one up, momentarily ignoring Pamela. Then she was beside him and they squeezed together, Tommy's long arm about her. They peered out, hearing Rollison's clear statement and his answers to the questions, seeing the crowd, sensing a mood of some hostility. Then the policeman had shouted:

"He's throwing a bomb!"

They saw the curious way the crowd seemed to sway back for the Toff, they watched as if hypnotised as the Toff caught the missile and, without a thought of nerves, threw it towards the empty house.

"Oh, *God!*" breathed Pamela.

Then Jolly cried: "Stop him, stop him!"

Tommy G. Loman looked away from the Toff and the bomb as the explosion flashed and roared, and saw a man pushing his way past two or three others, and saw, suddenly, a motor-cycle between two parked cars.

"*Stop that man!*" roared Tommy G.

"*Stop him!*" cried Jolly.

Pamela made herself look away from Rollison, who was flat on the ground, towards the man. Tommy was roaring: "Stop him, stop him!" and clutching her more tightly than she had ever been held in her life.

Two men broke from the crowd.

One was a policeman and the other was Ebbutt's man on that side of the street. The escaping man was only a few yards from the motor-cycle. He leapt towards it, straddled the seat and kicked the starter, but before he could move the machine Ebbutt's man was leaping at his back and the policeman pulling at his arm, until he was half on and half off the saddle. Motor-cycle and would-be rider collapsed against a car.

When all three men stood up the motor-cyclist was handcuffed to the policeman.

That was the moment when Tommy G. realised that his great hand was cupping Pamela's breast, not clutching her waist. It was the moment, too, when Pamela placed her hand over his as if to keep it there. And it was the moment when Jolly said in a trembling voice:

"Thank God he's all right. Thank God."

He meant Rollison, of course, who was being helped to his feet.

Yellow light from the fire already burning fiercely in the empty house shone on his face, making strange brilliance and dark shadow.

.   .   .

The television cameraman who wheedled his way into getting permission to install himself on the porch of a house had bemoaned his luck until the shout: "He's throwing a bomb!" The veering crowd, the movement of Richard Rollison from the running board of the T-model Ford, all came within his line of vision. He had special lights and highly sensitive film, and simply kept his finger on the 'take' button and the lens on Rollison.

He saw the explosion in vivid if miniature brilliance.

He saw Rollison moving like a Lilliputian, throwing himself down.

He heard the shouting: "Stop him!" and swivelled the camera and took pictures of the running men. They had disappeared from sight when he ran out of film, but he had so much that he could have danced for joy.

.   .   .

There were the viewpoints of the dozens of newspapermen; the still cameras and the 16 mm. held high above the photographer's head.

And there was Bill Ebbutt's view.

Ebbutt, a tall man, was nearer Rollison than any of the others, and nearer the explosion. He watched open-mouthed as Rollison caught the missile, even more open-mouthed as it was thrown unerringly into the front room of the empty house. He was the first to reach Rollison, and to see that he was no more than winded and bruised. It was no time at all before the flames began to roar, no time at all before the police were calling at houses nearby with warnings that the fire might spread. Remarkably soon, fire-engine sirens sounded in the distance and more police arrived, to cordon off the danger area. Most of the newspapermen were on their way back to Fleet Street, unable to put their stories in soon enough. Not a man among them failed to start with glowing tributes to the Toff.

An hour after he had left his flat, Rollison went up-stairs with Jolly just behind him; he had wanted Ebbutt to come up but Ebbutt pleaded that he must go home and tell his wife about the events of the past hour.

Half-way down the top flight of stairs was Pamela, her eyes glowing, and just behind her, stood Tommy G. Loman.

"Richard!" Pamela exclaimed, and hurled herself at Rollison. "You're not hurt, are you? Tell me you're not hurt!"

"All I need is some trifle," Rollison said lightly. "And I could do with a brandy as a chaser! No, I'm not hurt — barely a scratch here and there."

"Richard," said Tommy, quietly, "that was the bravest thing I have ever seen. And I've seen plenty. You expected an attack, didn't you?"

"If you or I appeared on the scene, yes," answered Rollison.

"Or Pamela," murmured Tommy, putting his arm

round Pamela's waist. "And you went to draw the man's fire."

"Thank heavens they caught him!" exclaimed Pamela.

"With a little luck a kind-hearted policeman will soon tell us whether he's talked," Rollison remarked. "Now I'm going to tidy up, while Jolly produces his dessert." He left them looking at him with expressions not far short of adulation, and went to his bedroom, then across to his bathroom. He swayed and held on to the hand-basin; the room seemed to be going round and round when Jolly came in, and without speaking, led him back to the bedroom and into an easy chair. Soon, Jolly had loosened his collar and tie, taken off his shoes and sponged his hands and face, his neck and forehead. After a while his head no longer went round and round and there was no drumming in his ears. At last, Jolly brought brandy.

"I must get back to the others," Rollison said.

"They are perfectly all right, sir," Jolly insisted. "They don't mind being left at all. If you really want a little trifle — "

"I shall stick to coffee and brandy," Rollison decided.

It was not long before, clad in a dressing-gown and wearing fleece-lined leather slippers, he went back to the big room. He did not know what had happened to Pamela and Tommy but they looked radiantly happy. Rollison lowered himself cautiously into his chair which gave him a comprehensive view of the room, and watched them with avuncular interest. The Regency star clock centred over the mantelpiece showed that it was half-past ten; as long an evening as he had ever known.

"You look better," Pamela said.

"I feel better," agreed Rollison. "I hadn't realised the excitement had knocked me silly. Have you two solved all our and the world's problems while I've been taking a snooze."

"*You* have," declared Pamela.

"Surely," said Tommy G. "The police are sure to make the prisoner talk, aren't they? And once he talks — "

"Even if he talks he may not know a great deal," Rollison pointed out. "But with luck we shall get news of Alec King in the morning."

Tommy nodded soberly.

"Every newspaper in the country will probably carry a picture of him," he observed. "Even before you proved what a good catcher you were, you were doing fine." He rose from his chair to his full enormous height, and went on: "Richard, I am going to walk Pamela home, so you can go to bed."

There was such positiveness in his voice that he obviously expected Rollison to object to his going out. Half of Rollison wanted to say "only a fool in your position would venture out tonight", but Pamela could be in as much danger as Tommy G. Loman and apparently these two young people had moved a long way from casual acquaintances in the past few hours.

"Tommy," he said. "I have bad news for you."

"Richard, I don't want to be difficult, but I — "

"You will have police behind you all the time," finished Rollison.

"Oh," said Tommy. "The cops." He grinned resignedly. "Sure. After what's happened I guess I can't expect anything else. Did you bring a wrap or a coat, Pam?"

"No," answered Pamela. "I hadn't expected to be so late."

"I'm sure Jolly can find you something," Rollison

offered. "If one of you will save my legs and press the bell by the fireplace — "

In a moment, Jolly appeared.

"If Miss Brown will come with me," he said, benignly, "she can select which wrap she would prefer."

He was out of the room with her when the front door bell rang.

Tommy turned towards it, half way out of the room and into the lounge-hall before Rollison had risen from his chair. Rollison did not know why he felt such sudden tension, was close to screaming point. On such a night anything might happen, men with such daring as the throwers of bombs might easily have charmed their way through the police cordon and be at the front door. One glance at the periscope mirror above the wall was all he needed to make sure.

He need not have worried.

"If you will allow me, sir," came Jolly's voice. Jolly must have nipped along the other passage, and he would not open the door without a glance in the periscope mirror. The sound of the front door opening followed and Jolly went on in a voice which, to the Toff's experienced ear, reflected some guarded pleasure. "Good evening, sir."

"Hallo, Jolly," said Chief Detective Superintendent Grice. "Is he all right?"

Rollison smiled and relaxed.

Grice came in, with Tommy who soon went back to Pamela Brown. Jolly appeared fleetingly to announce the policeman. Grice, as tall as Rollison, was still dwarfed by the man from Arizona. They were obviously wary of each other; as obviously Grice had not come to force any issue.

"One thing you can do is to have Mr. Loman and

Miss Brown followed, and Mr. Loman seen back safely here," Rollison said.

"I have already prepared for that with Mr. Ebbutt," said Jolly, coming in behind Pamela, "and the police will no doubt follow his men in turn."

"I should have known," said Rollison.

He watched Grice's expression when the policeman saw Pamela.

Obviously, it was one of recognition and there was a hint of surprise. Quite suddenly the others dropped into the background, while Grice and the girl looked at each other.

"Hallo, Miss Brown," Grice said at last. "Is your father better?"

"Thank you, yes," she said. "I didn't realise you knew he'd been ill."

"He was to have appeared as a witness in the South Western Court two days ago, and sent his apologies," said Grice. "I thought you'd been laid low, too."

"I was," said Pamela, smiling brightly. "Down first, up first."

"I must say it did you good," said Grice drily.

"*Thank* you, sir!"

"When this is over I shall want to know why you didn't come to the Yard with the whole story," Grice said, in a voice which he tried to make severe but did not wholly succeed.

"I'm sure Mr. Rollison will explain why," Pamela retorted. She was radiant as she turned to Rollison, and bent over and kissed him warmly on both cheeks. "Richard, you've been an absolute darling. Thank you, thank you, thank you!"

She was gripping his hands tightly when Tommy said:

"I echo them there sentiments, Richard."

He slid his arm through Pamela's and they went off; Jolly, with his uncanny ability to see everything that went on in the flat at once, was at the door to show them out. Grice leaned against the big desk, his back to the trophies, and looked at Rollison with a smile in his eyes and on his lips.

"And a matchmaker too," he teased.

"That young man is a much faster worker than he looks," Rollison said. "So you know the Browns."

"Very well. It's a family team and they specialise in tracing ancestors, family trees and that kind of research although they have taken on divorce work and searched for missing persons." Grice looked up as Jolly came in with coffee, cheese and biscuits on a tray — and the trifle, which looked most attractive in a cut glass bowl. "Rolly," Grice went on. "I am told you were magnificent."

Rollison waved his hands in silent disclaimer.

"And so will the newspapers, in the morning," went on Grice. "My men tell me they've never known such a change in the attitude of the Press. At first they thought you'd gone too far and scared Effie King into the premature delivery and they half-thought you'd caused the fire at her place. Now — " He spread his hands. "Are you up to talking."

"Not too long, sir, I beg you," pleaded Jolly.

"No, not too long," Grice promised.

"Thank you. Will you have some trifle, sir?"

"Do you know, it looks so tempting I believe I will," decided Grice, who had a notoriously sweet tooth despite his lean figure. "A little of that Cheshire cheese first, if I may."

Jolly ministered. Rollison stuck to coffee, and Grice simply asked: "Tell me all you know, Rolly. And if Jolly could tape it — ?"

Rollison leaned back, eyes half-closed, and remembered from the beginning, so short a time and yet so long ago. Everything that had happened was vivid in his mind, and he related the story with great lucidity while Jolly sat at the big desk with two small transistor tape recorders taking down every word. When the story was told, up to the moment when he had come back here and nearly collapsed, the second recorder tape had been used up. There was a sharp *click!* as Jolly switched the machine off.

Grice, who had finished eating, poured himself another cup of coffee as he remarked:

"The Browns were ill, and I suppose they can't be blamed for not coming to us about the old man's fears. We would have thought it a cock-and-bull story until Loman arrived at Heath Row and trouble really began. Taken at its face value, someone was planning to have Loman impersonated by King, who has now disappeared."

"That's how it seems to be," Rollison said. "And how it seemed once I knew the whole story."

"And you suspect this man Hindle, the man who expected to inherit?"

"He's an obvious suspect," Rollison said. "Do you know where he is?"

"I know he was supposed to have moved to a hotel, as his flat was uninhabitable after the firemen had finished with it," Grice said. "I'll check. And I know that King's wife Effiie has a son who is doing well. At seven pounds some ounces it doesn't seem very premature! She hasn't said a word and the doctor who attended her says she's suffering from shock as well as natural after-birth weakness, but she could be putting on an act so as to avoid being asked to tell us where her husband is."

"Yes," Rollison agreed warmly. "Have you a police-woman with her?"

"No, but I shall have, after this. Rolly — one thing above all puzzles me."

"I think I know what you mean," said Rollison. "Why go on with these murderous attacks now that the cat's out of the bag? No one could possibly hope to pull off the impersonation now. The first attempt at Kennedy Airport was viable, so was the one at Heath Row and even the attack on Rubicon House, because that destroyed the evidence that there is a planned impersonation. But tonight's attack seemed motivated by sheer malice. Has the prisoner talked?" he asked Grice.

"He simply says he was paid to make all three attacks by a man he's never seen — he gets his orders by tele-phone and knows the man only as A.M. There could be truth in this, and it will be difficult to prove he's lying. He's an ex-bomb disposal unit man who's lived by blowing safes for a long time, one of the psycho-pathic bad ones, I'm afraid. We'll keep trying but I doubt if we'll get much more from him. Well!" Grice stood up, briskly. "I'll go after Hindle and King, and if there are any results — "

"Let me know in the morning," pleaded Rollison.

Grice laughed: "I won't disturb you unless with epoch-making news! If I did, Jolly would never speak to me again, would you, Jolly?"

"No, sir," said Jolly with quiet vehemence. "Shall I make a copy of these tapes and let you have them?"

"Please. I — "

Grice broke off when the telephone bell rang, and Jolly, nearest to the instrument on the big desk, picked up the receiver and announced: "This is Mr. Richard Rollison's residence."

There was a moment's pause before he turned to Grice. "You are wanted back at the Station immediately, sir," he said gravely. "No, sir, the sergeant didn't say what for — only that it was a matter of utmost importance."

15

Attack

PAMELA BROWN HAD NEVER been so happy.

She knew that 'happy' was the right word, although what she felt was a kind of exaltation; euphoria. Whenever she felt Tommy's hands on her, it was as if an electric shock ran through her whole body. No one's touch had affected her in anything like the same way. She had known there was something different about the American when she had first seen him, and within an hour knew that he mattered. She even had time to try to rationalise. It was because of the excitement, the nerve-racking things that had happened, the fact that everything and everyone involved seemed so much larger than life.

Rollison, for instance: the Toff.

And that incredible scene when the bomb had been thrown.

Everything.

In spite of what had happened, and the known dangers surrounding them, so much had seemed funny. Persuading the police to let them pass the cordon to get her car, for instance! Dozens of firemen were directing water on the flames, and the fire was under control, but steam and smoke and the fat, snaking hoses made a kind of Bedlam. Then Tommy had tried to get at the wheel of the little car, and could not get his knees under it! So she had had to drive and he had to squat on the back of his seat, long legs stretched out. They said silly things; laughed; even giggled. She drove carefully to avoid making him bump his head, and kept her wits about her enough to know that they were followed by two cars.

It was half-past eleven when she turned into the drive of her house.

She had been born here, in a room in the shade of the trees of Clapham Common. It was a big, Victorian house standing on a corner, overlooking the Common on one side and the corner house across the street on the other. One of her father's prides was the shrubbery in the middle of the driveway; he, himself, clipped each laurel, rhododendron, privet and bush of every variety. Eric — her brother — took over only in emergency. Eric kept the grass trim and she looked after the flowers while her father was in sole charge of the small but fruitful vegetable garden behind the house.

As they had driven across Clapham Common, Tommy had been quiet almost for the first time, until he said wistfully:

"England sure is green."

"In daylight, this common is lovely," Pamela told him.

"Common?"

"Or park, I suppose you'd call it," she explained. "A patch of open land inside the city." She turned into the driveway, explaining: "I can put the car away afterwards."

"Where does it go?" he asked.

"In the garage."

"How do you get there?"

"Drive straight on to the side of the house."

"Is it dark in your garage?"

"It is if I don't put the light on," she said.

He bent down and kissed the side of her cheek. She fell silent as she drove on. Either her father or her brother had left the garage doors open, and the dipped headlights of the little car showed the shelves on one side, with tools and tins of paint and a few off-cuts of wood, with old tyres hanging on the wall at the far end. She drew the car to a standstill, and sat without moving. Tommy opened his door and eased his legs out.

"Come," he said.

She moved across to get out, and into his arms.

He held her so tightly that she could hardly breathe, but soon he let her go. He kept one hand on hers as they went out of the garage, for here there was no room for him to stand. Outside on the driveway, in the shadow of the laurels, he swung her round to face him and took her in his arms once again. She gazed up at him with a half-smile, and for a few moments they looked at each other without speaking; then, suddenly, Tommy bent his face to hers, and their lips met. Slowly, he drew her closer. She was wildly aware of him, desire was like fire in her veins as she knew it was in his. She felt her heart thumping as if it would burst through her ribs. She felt his hands, touching her, sending these currents of ecstasy through her whole body. His mouth found hers again, and for what seemed an age they were as close as one. Then, when at last he let her go, she gasped:

"Let's go — indoors."

"Can we?"

"Why not?"

Slipping her arm through his, she led him past the laurels and towards the house.

She heard no one approach, but then few noises would have sounded above their breathing. She saw no

one; but then all she could see was Tommy. Without
the slightest warning she felt a blow on the back of the
head, saw Tommy pitch forward as if he too had been
struck, suddenly felt her legs hooked from under her
and fell, her head cracking against a tree.

On that instant, she lost consciousness.

At the same time a man shouted from outside, and a
police whistle shrilled, but Pamela knew nothing of
what was going on.

.   .   .

Detective-Sergeant Williter, of New Scotland Yard,
had been standing by the side of his car, the driver still
at the wheel. It was a clear, starlit night, without a
moon. In the distance traffic hummed, in the sky aircraft droned on their ceaseless to-ing and fro-ing.
Ebbut's men were in a car round the corner, so that
both approaches to the house were covered.

"If you ask me," the driver said, "those two make a
bad case."

Williter nodded.

His job was to make sure the girl got home and that
the man returned to Rollison's flat safely, and no time
limit had been set for either. He was by nature both
patient and tolerant. When he saw the car disappear
into the garage, lighting up the inside, he waited; when
the car lights went out, he moved farther away. When
the couple lingered in the driveway, he moved back to
his car.

No one had told him to play gooseberry.

Out of the corner of his eye he saw a movement in
the shrubbery, and a moment later the figure of a man
appeared against the light-coloured gravel. He whispered to the driver:

"Come on, quick. Someone's there."

He was cut off from the garage by the shrubbery when there was a sudden gasp, a scuffle of movement. Williter put his whistle to his lips. Ebbutt's men came running from the side entrance and the police driver was close behind, shining a torch.

The beam fell on Pamela Brown, who lay still on the ground; on Loman, who was on his knees, his hands at his head, making a funny moaning sound, and on a man who was running alongside the garage towards the back of the garden.

"Stop him!" Williter roared.

Ebbutt's men were nearer, and could just make out the running man, now on the back lawn. One of them, a little terrier of a man, put on a spurt before flinging himself forward, hands outstretched for the runaway's ankles. He clutched one, and the man crashed down. Before he could get up, Williter had arrived and other policemen, summoned by radio from the division, were on the way.

When Williter returned to the path near the garage, grey-haired Martin Brown and his son were on their knees beside Pamela, and a policeman was bending over Loman.

"How is she?" Williter asked Brown, urgently.

"She's got a big bruise on the back of her head and bruises on her throat," Pamela's father said. "If I ever catch the swine who did it — "

"We've got him, and we'll take care of him," Williter retorted with deep satisfaction. He turned to the policeman who was straightening up from Loman; the American was no longer moaning but appeared to be trying to straighten out his legs. "How is he?"

"If you ask me," the policeman replied. "He had a knee or a kick in the groin, sir. You know what kind of pain *that* causes."

"I know," Williter said. "He'd better come with us to the Yard. Are you sure your daughter's all right?" he asked Brown.

"Yes," Brown growled. "No thanks to you, though." He glared at the prisoner, a short, solid-looking man with dark hair; there was something very un-English looking about him, he was more Southern European.

When at Scotland Yard this man was charged with assault with intent to cause bodily harm, he replied in a marked American accent — a New York accent to those who were familiar with accents from various parts of America.

"I didn't attack anybody. I was trying to help."

"What's your name?" Williter asked, and for an answer he had one of the shocks of his life.

"Sergeant Luigi Tetano, of the Long Island Police Homicide Squad," the arrested man answered; and so saying, he took his identifying badge out of his pocket.

.   .   .

Grice, who had hurried back to the Yard and been given news of the attack, went to the waiting room where the accused was being held. In the good light he saw the evidence of strain and tension on the plump face, the suppressed anger in the fine dark eyes. This man had much strength of character, and gave the impression of one with some authority who was fighting hard to maintain his self-control.

"I tell you I'm Sergeant Tetano," he insisted. "I came over on the same flight as Tommy Loman because I thought Loman was a victim of a luggage racket which has been causing trouble at Kennedy Airport for a long time. Too long," he added, scowling. "Then I began to wonder if I was wrong, so I stalled for a while, just watching. I was going to see what happened when the

Brown dame reached home. Sure, I knew she was on the way with Loman, I was in Gresham Terrace tonight during the shenanigan there, and stayed around until they left. I drove my rental car round the house while they were in the garage, and went into the yard on foot."

"Why?"

"I wanted to hear if they were in this together, they'd behaved like old lovers outside the garage, and — oh well, you don't need telling you have to suspect everybody. All I heard was a pair of lovebirds."

"And then?"

"Someone threw a rock at me," Tetano said, pointing to an inflamed swelling on his forehead. "I guess it was the man who attacked the others. By then your cops were closing in and I tried to get away."

"Why not stay behind and tell us what you've just explained?" demanded Grice.

"Are you kidding?" Tetano's voice rose in a laconic note. "Who was going to believe me?"

"It would have been easier to believe you if you stayed where you were," said Grice. "Did you get a good view of the assailant?"

"I didn't see a thing that mattered. One moment I was listening to the lovebirds and the next a rock hit me," answered the sergeant from Long Island Homicide. "Maybe that knocked the sense out of my head and I wouldn't have run if it hadn't hit me."

"Perhaps," Grice said. "Have you seen Mr. Loman before?"

"Sure — at Kennedy."

"Just one moment," Grice said. He went to the door, opened it, and stood aside for Tommy Loman to come in, and as the door closed he asked sharply: "Have you seen this man before, Mr. Loman?"

"Sure have," Loman replied without any hesitation.

"Where?"

"At Kennedy Airport," Loman said. "He's one of the cops there."

"Have you seen him in England?"

"No, sir, I have not."

"Did you see the man who attacked you and Miss Brown tonight?" asked Grice.

Loman replied in a wondering voice: "No, I didn't. I think the guy must have been hiding in the garage. All I know is something hit me in the groin and all I could think of was the pain. That was what I call *agony*. I didn't see who it was or what hit me. All I know is that if your men hadn't followed me, Superintendent, Pam and I both might be dead. How is she?" he added in a rougher voice.

"She'll be all right in a day or two," Grice tried to soothe.

"Are you sure, or —?"

"I am sure. She has been seen by her own doctor and by a police surgeon," Grice replied. "Are you going back to Gresham Terrace? Or would you rather stay here for the night? We could find you a shake-down."

"I promised Rollison I would go back."

"I'll have a car take you," Grice volunteered. He called for a man on duty outside, and gave instructions. Next he turned to Luigi Tetano and spoke in a more relaxed way. "Mr. Tetano, I am inclined to accept your statement but I'll need to keep you here overnight."

"On a charge?" Luigi asked, ruefully.

"No. Until I hear from Long Island."

"You'll hear the simple truth," Luigi assured him. "I thought it was the baggage racket and hopped the B.O.A.C. flight — all airlines will take a cop if he can prove he is one, and let him pay later. You will probably be told I'm absent without leave." After a pause, he went on: "You can't mean what I mean by a shake-down."

"A camp bed," Grice said. "The folding type. You surely have them in America."

"A camp — " Tetano started off puzzled and then exclaimed: "Oh, a rollaway! Why sure, that'll be fine! I didn't know Scotland Yard was a hotel."

Grice actually laughed.

"That Rollison," Luigi Tetano went on in a wondering tone. "He's quite a guy."

"Yes," agreed Grice quietly. "He is quite a guy. I only hope — " He broke off, as if suddenly reluctant to say what was in his mind.

"Hope what?" asked Luigi.

"That he lives through this case," Grice completed heavily, and looked the American straight in the eye. "I would hate him to die for a stranger he'd never heard of until this morning."

Luigi Tetano put his head on one side, and then asked softly:

"Are you sure of that, Superintendent? Are you sure Mr. Rollison has told you everything he knows or suspects in this case? Maybe you are but I am not. No, sir, I am not. I am a long way from it."

.   .   .

Oblivious of what had been going on, and of Luigi Tetano's doubts, Rollison slept the sleep of the sedated. It was Jolly who let Tommy into the flat, able to assure him that a police message had confirmed that Pamela Brown really was only slightly hurt.

Outside the police kept watch, while the empty house smouldered.

16

Hero!

ROLLISON WOKE TO VAGUE NOISES, turned over and blotted them out.

He woke again, to quiet, turned over and lay snug but did not get to sleep. Before long, he turned on to his back, and looked up at the ceiling; and as suddenly as new thought he remembered what had happened. He gave a little shiver. No one would ever know how much it cost to stand and wait for a little piece of metal which might blow one to smithereens. That shiver was the last of his conscious reaction to the previous night. He began to think, clearly and lucidly, about all that had happened. Glimmerings of ideas, not yet even half-formed, chased one another across his mind.

There was the obvious question: what was worth this series of vicious attacks?

A million pounds?

Yes, it could be; worse crimes had been committed for less reward, but there was a cold-blooded deliberateness about this affair which was rare.

What could be worth this series of vicious attacks?

His, Richard Rollison's, death?

Each attack had been on him —

That wasn't really true about the blowing up at Rubicon House. The grenade had been tossed into the first-floor flat to destroy the evidence, but at the airport and in Gresham Terrace there had been only one obvious purpose: to kill him.

Why?

What did he know?

What damage could he do to these desperate men?

He began to feel restless; it was time he was up and doing, finding out what else had happened, if anything; whether the newspapers had really gone to town in their hunt for Alec George King, whether the prisoner had changed his mind, and talked. With the telepathic understanding or awareness which had developed over the years, Jolly appeared silently at the door.

"Good morning, sir."

"Good morning, Jolly."

"I'll bring tea and the newspapers immediately, sir."

"Have they done us justice?" inquired Rollison.

"I think you will think so, sir." Jolly withdrew and Rollison hitched himself up on the pillows. Rain spattered the windows like tears from a thousand weeping giants, and the slate roofs of houses opposite glistened beneath grey skies. It was much colder than yesterday, too. He draped a dressing-gown round his shoulders as Jolly came in with the tea tray and several newspapers under his arm. This was one of Rollison's luxuries; tea and the newspapers, in bed.

"How is our guest?" he asked.

"Fully satisfied with the newspapers, sir!"

"Good. And you?"

"Very well and hopeful, sir."

"Better," remarked Rollison as Jolly poured tea and he opened the first newspaper: the *Globe*.

There he was, staring up at himself! And there was King, also on the front page, remarkably like Loman but with some noticeable differences — Loman's nostrils were wider, for instance. Beneath his photograph was the one word: *Hero.* Beneath King's there was the simple question: *Have you seen this man?* The story of what had happened at Rubicon House and at Gresham Terrace was vividly related, and inside were action photogarphs of the fire. He put the *Globe* aside, sipped hot tea and opened the *Echo.* Here, the action photograph was on the front page: there he was, hands cupped as if to catch a cricket ball, elbows tucked in close to his body; and there was the hand grenade, like a black egg! Someone must have been at the window of a house opposite to get such a picture.

Ten minutes later he put down the last newspaper and took his final swallow of now luke-warm tea. He had to wait only for a few moments before Jolly came back.

"Has Grice been calling?" asked Rollison.

"Yes, sir — he will be here at eleven o'clock."

Rollison shot a glance at a bedside clock, and relaxed. "So I've an hour."

"I came in as early as I did because I felt sure you would want to see him, sir. He had nothing to report. Three newspapers have been on the telephone to say they are inundated with reports from readers who say they've seen King, but of course there is no positive evidence yet. Mr. Grice *did* say that the man Hindle hasn't been found." Jolly allowed a decent pause, before asking: "Shall I run your bath?"

"Please. Has Mr. Loman had breakfast?"

"He elected to wait for you, sir," Jolly said.

Something in his manner warned Rollison that all was not yet well; or at least, that Jolly was holding something back. He would not do this for long, and would not delay at all if the matter were grave or needed immediate thought or action. Rollison pushed back the bedclothes, did a few muscle and lung stretching exercises in front of the window open to the rain, had his bath and shaved and dressed, all in twenty-five minutes. It was half-past ten exactly when he went into the big room, breakfast bacon and eggs murmuring on the hot plate and the appetising smell of coffee wafting from the dining alcove.

Loman was putting down the receiver of the telephone.

"Good morning," Rollison greeted.

"Hi," responded Loman, in a tone so flat that here, obviously, was the source of trouble. "Jolly says you had a good night."

"Oh, I did," Rollison said. "Come and have breakfast. You must be hungry."

"My stomach's flapping," agreed Loman, and they went to the table together.

Rollison fought back an impulse to ask what the trouble was, the bacon was crisp and the eggs as he liked them, each on a piece of fried bread: it was fascinating to watch how quickly Tommy demolished a huge plate of bacon and eggs. They were nearly through this main course before he said:

"Richard, you are more right than you know."

"Possibly," Rollison said. "I was once before, I'm told. What have I been prescient about now?"

"You shouldn't have let me take Pamela home last night."

Suddenly very still, Rollison asked: "Why not?"

Tommy told him the whole story, not once avoiding his gaze, and he finished by saying that he had just talked to Pamela's father, and learned that Pamela was awake, and apart from having a stiff neck and a lump on the back of her head, was unharmed.

"Someone tried to choke the life out of her," Tommy said bleakly. "He fixed me so that I didn't even know what was happening. If you hadn't made sure that the police and those friends of yours had followed, she would be dead. And I guess I would, too — he would have killed me after killing Pam."

"You may well be right but no one was killed or seriously hurt, and things could have been a lot worse." But the news added another question to those which already teased Rollison. Why try to kill him, why attack Pamela and Tommy, when it was so glaringly obvious that the impersonation attempt had failed?

Twice as they had been at the table the telephone bell had rung but Jolly had answered from the kitchen and not disturbed them. Now it rang again; and almost at once Jolly came in, to plug in a telephone so that Rollison could speak while at the table.

Rollison's eyes asked: "Who?"

"Mr. Ebbutt, sir," Jolly repeated.

"Ah, Bill!" Rollison spoke warmly into the telephone. "I hope you're all right after last night."

"Not so bad, Mr. Ar, not so bad at all," said Ebbutt, his wheezing very pronounced. "Glad to hear from his nibs that you're okay. Lucky you're not in Kingdom Come, if you don't mind me saying so. Mr. Ar, I got something on me mind about last night and I can't get it off until I talk to you."

"On the telephone?"

"If you could come over to the Blue Dog it would be better," Ebbutt said. "Lil's got a bad leg, Mr. Ar, and the doctor's coming to see 'er and I want to talk to him when he comes."

"I'll be over by one o'clock," promised Rollison.

"I'll be waiting for you," Ebbutt declared. "So long." Then he added hastily: "You'll come alone, woncher?"

"Yes," Rollison promised.

Ebbutt rang off, leaving Rollison mystified and un-easy. Ebbutt was usually the most open-minded and frank of men; why was he reluctant to say all he wanted to over the telephone? Rollison replaced the receiver as Tommy stood up and poured himself more coffee. Every time he stood to his full height it was startling. Rollison pushed his chair back and Jolly waited for both men to leave the alcove, then drew a curtain which divided it, when not in use, from the rest of the big room.

At eleven o'clock to the minute there was a ring at the front door bell, and Grice appeared on the periscope mirror. Rollison opened the door and sensed on the instant that Grice wasn't pleased with life. What on earth had gone wrong with everyone this morning? Grice stood close to Rollison as the door closed, and said in a whisper:

"I want to talk in confidence, Rolly, not with Loman present."

"If I know Loman, he will make his excuses as soon as you've said hallo," remarked Rollison. The feeling of uneasiness increased, for Ebbutt had said much the same thing.

Only Jolly was in the big living-room-cum-study.

"Mr. Loman has gone to his room," he informed them, "but he will be glad to join you if he should be needed."

"Thanks," said Rollison, and motioned Grice to a chair on the far side of the desk, while he sat in his padded swivel chair, back to the Trophy Wall. "I gather things went very badly last night," he said to Grice.

"I don't know how badly they went," said Grice, gruffly. "Rolly — answer a straight question."

"I will."

"Do you think Pamela Brown and Loman knew each other before they met here?"

"I do not," Rollison said flatly.

"Can you be sure?"

"No," Rollison admitted. "I can only say that the moment they met they seemed to be dazzled by each other. Why?"

"How well do you know Pamela?"

"Not at all," Rollison said. "You gave her and her father and brother a good reference last night though."

"She is occasionally used by the family business as a decoy," Grice told him. "She's a lovely-looking woman and can switch on charm like an electric current. I've never had the slightest reason to suspect her or her family of anything unlawful, but — "

"Decoy for what?" demanded Rollison.

"Oh, I'm sorry. A wife may come to the Browns for evidence of a husband's infidelity. Pamela gets to work on the husband. If he starts making passes then he's probably a man who will fall by the wayside with any attractive woman. If he doesn't but is seriously in love with someone else, then the Browns simply tell the wife they won't handle the case. Don't ask me to explain what makes them tick," Grice went on irritably. "I can only tell you what I know."

"I don't really see what you're driving at," Rollison protested.

"I'm not really sure myself," admitted Grice, ruefully. "Did Pamela make a dead set at Loman on meeting because she know's he's going to inherit the fortune? Or did she fall in love?"

"I don't know her well enough to be sure but I think she fell head over heels," answered Rollison. "I still don't see how this affects the main issue."

"I don't suppose you do," Grice growled. "I'm not

even sure it does. But I have an uneasy feeling that the Browns could be more deeply involved in this affair than I've suspected. Last night's attack could have been a fake."

"*What?*"

"The brother or the father could have attacked Loman and then Pamela," Grice said. "Her injuries are superficial, it could have been an attempt to convince us that she's in danger. Rolly, I just don't know!" Grice pushed his chair back and stood up. "But I'm worried out of my wits. There have been two attempts to kill you, and *they* weren't faked. The Rubicon House might have been mainly an attack on you, also. The Browns involved you, and their reasons are pretty specious. I have a feeling that I'm working in a nice, thick, smelly, pea-souper of a fog." He gave a short laugh as he approached the wall to a small shelf on which stood a single hobnail boot. "It was foggy in that case, wasn't it? I'd only just joined the force, and you were only just getting known."

"Bill," Rollison said quietly. "All fogs disperse sooner or later."

"Oh, yes." Grice turned back and leaned against a corner of the desk, closer to Rollison. "A man was picked up in the grounds of the Browns' house last night — an American policeman whose identity is beyond all doubt. He came over on the same flight as Loman because he thought Loman might be a victim of a big luggage stealing racket at Kennedy Airport. He really came on a kind of hunch. The thing is, Rolly — "

"Yes?" Rollison's voice was sharp.

"These are damned dangerous days. Hi-jacking of aircraft, the blowing-up of aircraft and government and police buildings are commonplace. We've got what looks like a case of impersonation to get a large inheritance, but the tactics used are the same tactics as those used by terrorists. Those hand grenades are now known to contain high explosive and powerful incendiary material much more powerful than they had originally. Can you tell me what's really going on, Rolly?" Grice asked, and then leaned forward and demanded in a hard voice: "If you have the faintest idea you've *got* to tell me. You can't fight a war against terrorists on your own."

17

Ebbutt Warns

ROLLISON WAS SO STARTLED that he sat back sharply enough to bump his head against a hangman's rope which dangled on a swivel; someone had moved it from the wall. He half-turned, pushed it back, then faced Grice again.

"No," he said. "I can't and I know I can't. I have seldom, if ever before, been involved in a case about which I've told you everything from the beginning."

"Everything?" Grice echoed, dubiously.

"Everything. Bill, this may be an offshoot of a baggage racket at Kennedy Airport. It could be an extension of terrorist activities — it had the look of that from the beginning, but if it is, I've no advance knowledge of it. And we may have a simple case of attempted fraud on a scale big enough to warrant all the violence. Did Jolly give you that tape yesterday?" he added abruptly.

"Yes."

"That is everything I can tell you," Rollison asserted.

"But it doesn't make sense," protested Grice. "They *are* trying to kill you."

"I was vaguely aware of that," Rollison retorted. When Grice did not respond, he asked: "Have you learned anything from the prisoner?"

"He is a man named Simms, much older than he

looks when he's on his motor-cycle," Grice replied.
But he can't, or won't, give us any help. He lives in
a one-room apartment in Notting Hill, and had twenty-
one more of the grenades stacked in a cupboard. He's
admitted the attacks, denies that he is being paid by
anyone and says he's a revolutionary who thinks that
everyone who lives in Mayfair should be executed."

"Do you believe him?"

"No. But it could be true."

"Did he say why he threw the bomb at Rubicon
House?"

"He says he followed you and had seen you in the
room."

Rollison felt a shiver run down his spine.

"I hope there aren't many more about like him," he
said, heavily. "Is there any word at all about Hindle?"

"No."

"Or the actor, King?"

"No."

"How's his wife?" asked Rollison.

"She's still under sedation," answered Grice. "She
came round once, and said she didn't know where her
husband was, she hadn't seen him for two days. The
baby is perfectly normal in every way according to the
doctors and nurses," he went on with a faint smile. "We
still haven't a line on King, although we're keeping a
teletype machine and five telephones open for com-
munication with the newspapers, who are being inundated with calls from people saying they've seen him in
a hundred different places at the same time. One or two
are from people who've known him in the theatre or
socially, and we're following these up, of course."

"Yes," Rollison said, heavily.

"What's on your mind?" asked Grice, and when
Rollison didn't answer immediately he went on: "Do

you think they killed him once they knew the switch of individuals couldn't work? So that he wouldn't be able to talk, I mean."

"It's possible," Rollison admitted.

"It's everything I would have called melodramatic nonsense," said Grice. "More American than British."

"After the Kray brothers and the Great Train Robbery I don't see how we can say that," objected Rollison.

"Is there anything else at all you can tell me?" asked Grice, tacitly accepting defeat on that.

"Nothing, but Bill Ebbutt telephoned in a mysterious mood, wanting me to go and see him," Rollison told the Yard man. "One of his chaps might have picked something up. I'm going over to find out."

"It's a waste of time saying 'be careful'," Grice sighed, standing up slowly.

"It's probably not even possible in this affair," replied Rollison.

He saw Grice out, then went back to the big room to find Tommy G. Loman coming from the passage which led to his room, a savage look on his face. Rollison thought for a moment that he was annoyed because Grice had not seen him, but the tall man said in a voice cold with anger:

"I called Pam's father, and can you imagine what he said?"

"What did he say?"

"He said if I go anywhere near his daughter he'll horsewhip me."

Rollison, smiling faintly, said: "I would like to see him try," and rested a hand on the bony shoulder. "It's bad enough as it is, I know, and worse because you can do nothing. All the same, I would prefer you to stay here. You might hear from a newspaper which really has a clue where we can find King."

Scowling, Tommy said: "You want to know something, Toff? I'm not staying in this apartment for ever."

Rollison gave a mock shudder and said: "Heaven forbid!"

Tommy was actually laughing when Rollison went out.

Police and a few newspapermen were still in the street, and the windswept rain brought a faint odour of burning from the house which had been destroyed. A small fire tender and some firemen were outside the house. Rollison evaded the newspapermen but not the police, and went to the mews garage where the battered Bristol had been taken after the fire. The engine started at a touch, and he drove to Piccadilly and then through the heart of London to the East End. The heavy rain and gusty wind made driving unpleasant. He kept a police car in view in his driving mirror, and had no doubt that policemen along the route were on the alert for him and would report his progress to the Yard's Information Room. Once through the narrow streets of the City, past the great banking houses and the insurance companies, the Bank of England and the Stock Exchange, he drove through surprisingly light traffic through Aldgate and then the Mile End Road.

The police car kept close behind.

Policemen waved him on.

Soon he was in a section of old London's dockland, where narrow streets of tiny houses without gardens looked drab as well as dank. At last he turned a corner where there was a big Victorian public house, The Blue Dog; an inn sign with a blue greyhound on it swung and groaned in the wind. He pulled round the corner, to a wooden building standing back from the road, emblazoned:

EBBUTT'S GYMNASIUM

Here, over the years, Bill Ebbutt had trained some of the best boxers of the British ring.

A little man with his coat collar turned up against the rain came hurrying towards Rollison, peaked cloth cap sodden.

"In the pub, Mr. Ar!" he called, and led the way to the backyard of the Blue Dog where huge barrels and stacks of beer bottle crates made a kind of maze. The back door opened as they appeared and Ebbutt stood beaming at his visitor, then gripped his hand.

"How's the conquering hero this morning?" he inquired in a wheezy whisper. "Come in, Mr. Ar." He led the way to a parlour at the back of the main bars. On the table were two tankards, in a corner a wooden barrel, marked XXXX — the best beer brewed in Britain, Ebbutt claimed. It stood on a trestle made of unpolished oak.

As he turned the faucet, and raised and lowered the tankards to get the proper head of beer, he said:

"Lil's asleep — sprained her ankle and the doctor gave her a sedative." He handed Rollison his tankard and raised his own, his small eyes sparkling in anticipation. "Here's to the conquering hero," he toasted. "Blimey, that was a job you did last night, Mr. Ar."

"Bill," said Rollison. "I'm sure you didn't ask me here just to tell me how brave I am."

Ebbutt's expression changed. He drank more beer, wiped his lips with the back of his hand, and slowly shook his head. Rollison waited in the now familiar mood of disquiet.

"Mr. Ar," Ebbutt said, "I don't trust that Pamela Brown."

"Oh," said Rollison, taken completely by surprise.

"I don't trust her no farther than I can see her," Ebbutt went on. "She's a living doll all right, they don't come any prettier and I don't say that when I was younger I wouldn't have liked a date or two with her. But I don't trust her an inch." Ebbutt drank again and repeated the motion of wiping his mouth with the back of his hand. "She did a job on old Sonny Tucker, two or three years ago. He'd been out on the old razzle-dazzle and his wife wanted evidence. You know the kind of thing. Pamela Brown got everything out of the poor old geezer, where he'd been, who he'd been with."

"Did his wife divorce him?"

"Divorce? Who said anything about divorce? Old Sonny's been under his wife's thumb since that very day." Ebbutt squeezed his huge bulk in a shabby old armchair, and went on above the wheezing in his chest; it was almost as if there were two men inside him; or Ebbutt and his echo. "Well, your American buddy has fallen for her hook, line and sinker, hasn't he?"

"How do you know?" asked Rollison.

"My boys keep their eyes open," Ebbutt said, "and all I can tell you is that she's up to no good. You take my word for it." Ebbutt drained his tankard before going on: "I couldn't come and see you, seeing as Lil was laid up, and telephones 'ave ears."

Rollison said slowly: "And your boys have eyes."

"That's right," said Ebbutt, clasping the arms of his chair with fat hands. His tone and his mood changed again. "All I can say, Mr. Ar, is you be very careful where those Browns are concerned. They're dynamite."

The word seemed to hover in the air. There was no doubt Ebbutt had used it deliberately; the steady gaze, the sombre expression, told Rollison that. Pamela Brown was dynamite.

"Bill," Rollison said, "are you telling me that you

seriously think the Brown family could be behind the bombing?"

"All I know is that I wouldn't trust any one of them an inch, and I wouldn't trust your American friend with them, either. Beauty's only skin deep, that's what I always say." Then Ebbutt leaned forward, both hands outstretched, and his manner as well as the tone of his voice were beseeching.

"Be careful, Mr. Ar. That wasn't funny last night. You was about ten seconds, maybe less, between staying in one piece and being blown to smithereens. I don't want nothing to happen to you, Mr. Ar. It turned me inside out when I realised what was happening."

Ebbutt paused, then spread his hands, then added with great depth of feeling:

"Can't you give this one up. Get out while you've still got a whole skin? A hell of a lot of people would breathe a lot easier if you'd drop out. Mr. Ar. I've never said a truer word."

.   .   .

First Grice. Then Ebbutt.

If he didn't know them better he would think they had been in collusion over this; if by chance they had then each believed beyond all doubt in the acuteness of his danger.

But even if he wanted to, how could he 'give this one up'? He didn't really know what it was, yet in all that had happened there must be the vital clues which, when seen and properly understood, would explain everything.

Why *had* the Browns told Tommy Loman to go to him? Clearly, so as to involve him. Was Pamela's explanation right or was there another? Was there the slightest possibility that there had been a faked attack on her by one of her family? If so, what possible reason could there be?

Or would Brown Senior threaten to choke the life out of him, too?

Rollison, sitting at the wheel of the Bristol in dense traffic near the Bank of England, with the stench of car exhaust fumes and the growl of car engines all about him, went very still. The car behind him honked, and he realised a light had turned green. He drove on, going towards Blackfriars Bridge and the Embankment, the quickest way to Fleet Street. He found a parking place between *Evening News* delivery vans and as he did so a car drew up alongside him.

His heart lurched until he realised that the driver was Grice's man.

"Where are you going, Mr. Rollison?" he asked, severely.

"To the *Globe* newsroom — I want to find out if they've any news of King."

"If we lose you we can't be responsible for what happens."

"No," agreed Rollison. "I hereby absolve you. Why doesn't one of you come along and hold my hand?"

"That's exactly what we'll do," the driver replied, and his companion got out on the other side.

Rollison and a massive, black-jowled detective officer walked together along narrow streets, past huge, old-fashioned buildings, to the *Globe* offices in a side street. They went upstairs to the newsroom together and the Yard man looked dubious when the News Editor, an old acquaintance, carried Rollison off to a sanctum sanctorum, small, choc-a-bloc with hide armchairs, and a huge desk along one side.

"Rollison," said the News Editor, whose name was

Green, "we have undoubtedly narrowed down the search for this actor, King."

Rollison's heart began to beat fast.

"Beyond any doubt?"

Green, a very thin, very sharp-featured man with a high dome of a forehead, answered without hesitation:

"Beyond doubt. He's been in a television series recently and one of the cameramen on the crew which makes the show lives in Clapham. He's seen King drive to Clapham Common several times. A woman who watches the show regularly lives in a flat in a house overlooking Clapham Common; she says she saw King go into a corner house opposite the Common yesterday morning. He'd been there two or three times before. She's certain because she's been dithering about whether to waylay him and ask for his autograph."

Rollison asked, bleakly: "Any other evidence?"

"We've had a greater concentration of reports that he's been seen in the Battersea and Clapham Common area than anywhere else," Green told him. "And so have the *Echo* and the *Record*. I don't think there's much doubt."

"The house is the Browns' house, of course," Rollison said.

"Yes."

"Thanks," said Rollison. "Give Bill Grice a call at the Yard and tell him I hope to see him within half an hour. It will depend on the traffic whether it takes any longer."

"I'll tell him," promised Green, and as they stood up he went on: "May I add my word to the thousands you must have had about last night? My men who were there were converted from sceptics to convinced Toffophiles in a matter of seconds."

Rollison made his usual gesture, a self-disparaging wave of his hands in front of his chin. "I'm serious, believe me," Green insisted. He walked to the lift with Rollison, picking up the massive detective officer on the way. "Be careful, won't you?" he said as the lift doors opened. "You're not a man we want to lose."

18

The Browns' House

"Now you can see for yourself," Grice said.

He stood by Rollison's side in a small room on the same floor of the Yard as his office, in front of a map of London which was pasted on panels and hung on one wall. A door behind them was open and the clatter of typewriters and the chatter of men's voices came through clearly. A man on one side held a box of colour-headed pins in one hand; as each new report of King having been sighted came in, he stuck in another pin.

By far the largest concentration was in the Battersea and Clapham area, and easily the thickest grouping of brown-headed pins was at a spot on Clapham Common. The common was shown in green, and all the streets nearby in black and white; and individual houses were shown as tiny rectangles or squares. At least fifty pins were clustered near that spot. Some distance away, nearer the heart of London, were other groupings, one near Rubicon House, Chelsea, and one at the converted theatre where the television series was made.

"We don't stick a pin in unless the report seems convincing," said Grice. "For every one you see here the newspapers must have had twenty other reports. There can't be any doubt, Rolly; King is at the Browns' house where he's often been before. No wonder Loman was warned off!"

"No wonder," echoed Rollison. "Any word of Hindle?"

Grice said softly: "Some reports, yes." He pointed to some ordinary steel pins without coloured heads, which were also clustered near the Browns' house. "Reports that a man answering Hindle's description have come fairly frequently. Seven reports — as you see there are seven pins — seem reliable. If they are, Hindle and his wife went to the Browns' home about an hour and a half after the fire at Rubicon House yesterday afternoon."

"Well, well," Rollison said, heavily.

"So," said Grice, "we shall move in."

Rollison looked at him broodingly.

"Must you?" he asked.

"What a thing to ask! Of course we must. Hindle must be questioned about employing the motor-cyclist, and King — " Grice broke off. "It's true there's no evidence except yours that King is involved, and yours is circumstantial, but he has to be questioned."

"Yes," said Rollison, and then with a great effort: "Indubitably."

Grice gave him a long, sour look.

"What's on your mind?" he demanded.

"Hand grenades," Rollison replied.

Grice made no comment.

"Presumably you have the house cordoned off," Rollison went on. "Presumably at a given signal your men will move in. How many? Ten? Twenty? Thirty?"

"At least thirty," Grice said, uneasily.

"How many casualties do you think you'll have?"

"We shall take every possible precaution," Grice growled.

"Soothing for the widows," observed Rollison.

"Rolly, we have reason to believe two wanted men who may be responsible for these murderous attacks are in the house, and that the Browns are giving them shelter. We simply have to go in."

Rollison looked at him levelly, and after a while said very quietly:

"It will be a mistake, Bill."

"You simply don't understand!" Grice insisted, and now his voice was very rough. "If there are more grenades and fire bombs in that house, if the Browns are the distributors, we have no time to spare."

"You could ask for military help," Rollison pointed out.

"And perhaps create a crisis situation."

"Yes," Rollison said. "Yes. Bill."

"No," Grice growled.

"Bill," Rollison repeated, "you don't really have a choice. If some scatterbrained private individual is prepared to visit the Browns' house and look round, you have to let him. No policeman could be sent on his own — you know that perfectly well. One policeman is too many. But they would let me in."

"There is no evidence at all that they would let you out."

"No," agreed Rollison. "However — I think I have one rod ready for them which might pickle nicely."

"Rolly," Grice said with absolute decisiveness. "I will not let you go."

"Bill," Rollison replied, very quietly, "you know perfectly well you can't stop me. I can go where I like as a private individual. You have no grounds at all for detaining me. Have you?"

Grice did not reply.

"You know you haven't," Rollison went on as quietly

as before. "But I don't want Jolly to know where I've gone — nor Tommy Loman, who will tell Jolly and will also want to come with me."

"I'd rather he went than you," Grice growled.

"But he could not hope to do any good."

"Rolly, if these are the people who have been throwing bombs at you, you are walking right into their arms."

"My strength," Rollison declared.

"I don't follow you."

"You're too worked up about this affair," Rollison told Grice, gently reproachful. "You aren't letting yourself think clearly. They will know that you will know I've gone there, and if they don't let me out, then it's a declaration of war on the police."

Grice said: "They may take the chance."

"Yes," Rollison said. "They may. It really depends on what the affair is all about." After a few moments he went on: "There's no reason why we shouldn't have a time limit. Say, an hour from the time I go inside. And there's every reason why we should lay some careful plans before I go in. By the way, may I see this New York policeman, what's his name?"

"Luigi Tetano."

"That's the chap."

"Why?" asked Grice.

"I'd like to find out other evidence he has to suggest that the doping of Tommy Loman might have been connected with the baggage racket," Rollison said, and suddenly gripped Grice's shoulder. "Bill, I've walked into trouble as ugly as this a dozen times."

"I don't think so," Grice objected. "I do think — "

"Well?"

"I think you know something these people fear becoming common knowledge," Grice said. "It's the only reasonable explanation of the way they've set out to kill you. Are you sure you don't know what it is?"

"I don't have the faintest idea," Rollison answered. "Yet."

He had a sense that Grice had acknowledged defeat, and was not going to fight any more; he also suspected that when Grice took him back to his office and went out, ostensibly to fetch Luigi Tetano, he was also going to talk to his superiors. Rollison waited by the window which overlooked Victoria Street, seething now with traffic. The rain had stopped and the sun shone fitfully, while the sky between the breaks in the white cloud was a vivid blue. Very soon, Grice came back with the American, who advanced slowly towards Rollison, saying:

"Mr. Rollison, I'm proud to meet you."

"Oh, dear," Rollison said. "That's always an intimidating way to begin. Did you really hop that plane without permission, just to follow your hunch?"

"Yes," answered Luigi. His eyes had the brightness of a doe's, his cheeks were soft and sallow, pale; like a woman's. He had a bow-shaped, gentle-looking mouth.

"Then *I'm* proud to meet *you,*" Rollison said, as they shook hands.

Luigi laughed: "Thank you!"

"Lieutenant — "

"Sergeant."

"Sergeant, why was your hunch so strong? Why did you think this cowboy from Tucson had special significance?" He saw Grice go out, and only essential business would have taken Grice away at that particular moment. The American rubbed his chin with his thumb and forefinger before replying:

"I don't know, Mr. Rollison. I simply don't know. Except — " He paused.

"Except what?"

"Except it seemed to me he might have something very special in his baggage for them to give him a shot and make sure he didn't wake up in time to prevent them from claiming it."

"Nothing else at all?" asked Rollison. He had not really expected more, and yet he was disappointed. He liked the other man, could well believe that he had taken the chance exactly as he had said, and yet . . .

"Mr. Rollison, the whole set-up seemed phoney," Tetano declared at last. "It seemed to me they might be drawing attention to this cowhand while they were doing something else, and I wanted to find out what the something else was. That's one reason I am so mad, I allowed him to be doped in the B.O.A.C. plane, but when I saw him in his seat I got out quick to see if I recognised any of the other passengers. I didn't and came to the conclusion it was not part of the baggage racket. Now maybe I wonder if it has anything to do with these bomb-throwings. And I guess — " his eyes crinkled at the corners as he went on: "I wondered if you know more about it than you admit."

"So Bill Grice has been talking," Rollison remarked.

"Yes, sir, he has been talking," replied Tetano. "He seems to think you are a cross between a saint and Machiavelli. He lives in a state vacillating between being frightened of what you'll do next and being frightened for you."

"Just between you and me," said Rollison, "I think I'm a little frightened for myself, too."

He looked up as Grice returned, pale-faced; shook hands with Luigi Tetano, who went out with a chief inspector who followed Grice in, then raised his hands in a hopeless kind of gesture.

"Still of the same mind?" Grice demanded.

"Yes, Bill."

"I've instructions not to try to stop you if you're set on going into the place," announced Grice. "And not to encourage you, either. Rolly, I'd a thousand times rather go myself."

"I know you would," replied Rollison. "But if they are what you fear they are, they wouldn't let you in. They will let me in — and they may even let me out. One thing, Bill, or rather two."

"Anything."

"First, don't let Tommy Loman out of my flat," said Rollison. "He could go to the Browns' house and ruin everything." Grice nodded. "Second, don't let Luigi Tetano leave the Yard until you hear from me." Grice looked surprised, but nodded again. "Now!" went on Rollison briskly. "I have half a dozen tear-gas cigarettes and one palm gun. Wish me luck!"

"Luck," Grice almost groaned.

Rollison went downstairs. His Bristol was parked just round the corner, in Broadway, with two policemen watching it. No one made a move as he got in; no one followed as he pulled off and drove away. It was almost strange not to be followed by a police car. Traffic was still thick but the roads were drying except for pools in the kerbs, and there was a freshness even in the fume-laden streets, unbelievable freshness in Clapham Common, rising from the rain-soaked grass and the glistening, rain-wet leaves. He drew near the Browns' house but did not turn into the drive. Instead he pulled in at the first available parking space along the street, and walked back. With the contrariness of autumn, the sun was shining low but brightly, and the air was warm and sticky; he was glad he had not brought a raincoat.

He turned into the house drive, and studied the garage, where the assault had been made. The rain had drowned or muddied all clues, brown and yellow and golden leaves were on the damp gravel. The M.G. was where the girl had left it the night before.

There *was* something left behind; a vital clue, somewhere.

Tucked between the garage door and the wall of the house was a small black dress bag, with a *petit point* rose in pale pinks and whites and blues. That was where it must have fallen when she had been attacked. He felt the familiar shudder go through him, but did not pick the handbag up. He turned back to the arched portico of the front door, with freshly painted sides and colourful tiles on the floor. The door itself was jet black, the knocker, bell-push and letter-box old-fashioned brass; it needed cleaning.

He pressed the bell but could not hear the ringing.

People passed in the street; cyclists passed; and motorists. But all of them seemed far off and remote, although they were within earshot. He heard footfalls on the other side of the door, heard the handle turning, next a faint creak as the door opened. A man in his late twenties stood there, sufficiently like Pamela Brown for Rollison to think: it's her brother. The man was pale and uneasy.

"I'm Richard Rollison," Rollison said, pleasantly. "I've come to see how Miss Brown is. I do hope she's better."

"She — she is all right," replied the other. "I'm her brother. Please — " he seemed to gulp. "Please come in."

He stood to one side.

Beyond him was a large hall, with a streak of vivid sunlight coming through on one side and what looked like the shadow of a man's head and shoulders against the light where it struck a wall of pale-colour. Rollison could see a staircase, rising on one side; this much wider than most, with oil paintings, furniture and tall doors.

He stepped inside.

Before he was past young Brown, before he could see clearly about the hall, a man cried in a hoarse, penetrating voice:

"Get out, get out! They'll kill you! Don't come in!"

Several things happened at once.

A man, out of sight until then, slammed the door so that Rollison was shut inside, and at the same moment gave young Brown a savage kick which made him gasp, stagger, and fall. Another man, at the head of the staircase, began to fall. Rollison could not see more than his tumbling figure but he felt sure this was the older Brown. This man reached the bottom of the stairs and fell in a heap, breathing heavily, and making no attempt to get up. Still another man appeared at the head of the stairs, holding a gun. He was *Hindle!* And although he did not look round Rollison sensed that the man who had been behind the door also had a gun.

Hindle reached the foot of the stairs and said, sneering: "Come into our parlour."

"Said the spider to the fly," Rollison capped with hardly a pause. "And before either of you make the mistake of using a gun on me, let me remind you of the oldest and simplest trick of all. I left a letter with the Editor of the *Globe* this afternoon, to be opened only if I died. I assured him it meant nothing while I was alive but would be the scoop of his lifetime if I were to die by violence today, or even fail to reappear by eight o'clock this evening. But you must be businessmen as well as rogues," he added, lightly. "As businessmen, why don't we talk?"

19

Business

CLEARLY, HIS REMARK was the last thing either of the men expected. Hindle, stepping from the shadows at the foot of the stairs, was suddenly struck by a shaft of sunlight which turned him into gold. The brilliance dazzled him. If ever there was a chance to turn the tables it was now, but Rollison did not attempt to, and the man from behind the door ordered:

"Don't move."

Young Brown was now in a huddled heap on the floor. His father still lay, unmoving, at the foot of the stairs. He might be unconscious; or he might be dead of a broken neck.

Hindle stepped out of the vivid light, into the shadow; and he became again a grey shadow of a man.

"Talk?" he echoed. "What have we to talk about?"

"Enough," Rollison said.

Hindle stared, puzzled, but did not move his gun, and Rollison was right in the line of fire. Except for young Brown's gasping there was no sound, until suddenly a thud came from upstairs, footsteps sounded, a door banged. At the head of the stairs, Pamela Brown appeared; another shaft of sunlight struck her face, so that it seemed to make a physical barrier she could not pass.

"Watch her!" Hindle ordered the man by the door.

"Oh, Daddy, Daddy!" Pamela cried, and she ran downstairs through two of the shafts of sunlight, a beautiful vision. She flung herself by the side of the man on the floor, and began to talk to him, urgently, fiercely. "Don't die, oh, please don't die." She had his head in her lap and her forefinger was on his wrist. "He needs a doctor," she cried. "You must send for a doctor!"

Hindle rasped: "Shut up." He was looking at the Toff, when he went on: "Come on, tell me. What have we got to talk about?"

"The split," Rollison said.

"*The split*," breathed Pamela in a horrified voice.

"Are you crazy?" Hindle rasped.

"Not yet," Rollison said. "There are several of you, including your wife. I'll go sixty-forty. You have the sixty."

"You *are* crazy!" cried Hindle.

"It doesn't matter whether I'm crazy or not," Rollison said. "If I'm not out and about, free as the air, at eight o'clock this evening, the *Globe* will know where to find Alec George King."

Hindle drew in his breath, as if something hurt him.

"He's not here, no one could find him."

"After what's happened this morning, no plea of innocence will help you. If King isn't here you know where he is." Rollison paused before going on: "For a forty per cent cut I'll keep my information to myself, but always with a 'to be opened on my death' letter with my bank manager. You'll have to pray that I live long enough for you to enjoy your share."

From behind Rollison the younger man breathed: "Who would believe *this*?"

From her father's side, Pamela Brown said in a whispering tone which held horror tinged with unbelief:

"Oh, no, no, no. Not *you*." She was staring at the

Toff, her eyes filling with tears. The new shock had superseded even that caused by her father's crumpled body.

Rollison said in a brisk voice: "Don't be silly, Pamela. You're a big girl now. If you want to help your father, straighten his body and his arms and legs and check for broken bones. You needn't worry, all you and your precious family have to do is keep quiet."

"Oh, dear God," Pamela said huskily; but at least she began to do as she was told, easing her father's head from her lap and gradually straightening his body. He lay limp, and did not open his eyes or utter a sound.

Hindle breathed: "Was I wrong about *you*, Toff."

"A lot of people are wrong about me," Rollison said, off-handedly. "You can get away with this and sixty per cent of the Clayhanger inheritance, or you can get away with nothing. Even the satisfaction of killing me won't help."

"You can't have known we were involved," said Hindle, with a catch in his voice.

"Of course I knew," Rollison replied testily. "If you weren't pretty certain that I realised what you'd done, why should you be so intent on killing me? The bombing was as effective a way as you could think of, and distracted the police who thought I was involved with a terrorist organisation."

"They *did*!"

"They did. Tell me," said Rollison. "How did you get hold of the motor-cyclist?"

"He's a friend of my son."

"Your son? This chap?" For the first time, Rollison turned to look at the man who had been behind the door and who was still covering him with a gun. "You really meant to keep it in the family, didn't you?"

"That's where it belongs," Hindle said, waspishly.

"Pop," said young Hindle, "he's talking too much."

"I don't know, Derek," said Hindle, slowly. "If he's telling the truth — "

"I'm telling the truth," Rollison interrupted.

Out of the corner of his eye he saw young Brown move. He did not know whether the Hindles saw it, and waited, watching Hindle and seeing the girl who was now beyond him. She was smoothing her father's forehead, and there was no way for Rollison to know how the man was. But when she glanced up the loathing in her eyes, at sight of him, showed just how she felt towards the man whom she had virtually hero-worshipped.

So, he had convinced her.

He thought he had convinced the Hindles. If he had, then he still had a chance in spite of the two guns. But if young Brown leapt at Derek Hindle he, Rollison, would not have a chance; shooting would start.

He caught a glimpse of young Brown, face turned towards him. That face resembled Pamela's even more, perhaps because the expression of loathing for him, the Toff, was exactly the same. And young Brown was beginning to tense himself, to make some move.

Rollison said roughly: "Watch Brown!"

Derek swung round as the other tried to scramble to his feet, but Brown did not have a chance. For an awful moment Rollison thought Derek would shoot him; instead, he took two long strides and kicked him, savagely. Pamela cried out. Her brother fell back, in agony, Derek Hindle grinned as if the act of causing pain had given him pleasure.

Then Pamela flung herself on Hindle.

He was taken so much by surprise that she was able to grip his gun arm and twist. He yelped with pain and the gun flew from his grasp. Pamela darted towards it, and at that moment Rollison could have dealt with Derek, could have turned the tables completely. Instead, he moved with startling speed across the room and reached the gun, kicked it out of Pamela's reach, and, when she turned and flew at him, eyes blazing, trying to scratch his face, gripped her so tightly that the breath actually hissed out of her body. For a split-second his lips were close to hers and he whispered:

"Keep this up. I need half an hour."

For a scarcely perceptible moment she went still; then suddenly she became a screaming, writhing shrew of a woman, kicking, kneeing, clawing, scratching, until at last Derek Hindle pulled and flung her away.

Rollison dabbed a cut in his cheek, watching Derek frogmarch the girl to a cupboard under the stairs and the father force young Brown to the same place. There was a vicious streak in Derek Hindle; he slammed the door to try to catch young Brown's fingers, but Brown snatched them away in time. All the men now in the hall were breathing hard — except Brown senior, who lay so still. Rollison went down on one knee and felt his pulse.

"Forget the old fool," Derek rasped. "He hasn't long to live, anyhow."

"Someone ought to tell your son Derek that you can buy silence, you don't have to kill," Rollison said.

"You couldn't buy the Browns," retorted Hindle.

"They'd keep quiet if their daughter was married to Thomas G. Loman of Tucson, Arizona, heir to a million-plus-pounds, not dollars." Rollison infused some lightness into his tone. "Everyone involved will keep quiet. You two have to get out of the country soon — presumably you have false passports?"

"We've got it all arranged," said Hindle.

"How much do the Browns know?"

"Nothing that matters, except that we took their house over, and what's happened today," Hindle answered.

"What made you come here?" asked Rollison.

"We didn't know how much Pamela Brown knew and had to find out. And knowing you, we thought you would probably come to see her in your great hero act." Hindle gave a cackle of laughter.

"What about —?" began Rollison.

"To hell with your questions!" rasped Derek Hindle. "Pop, I say he's lying."

"I shouldn't put it to the test," Rollison warned.

They stood in silence for a few moments which seemed to drag out into minutes, and when a sound came it surprised Rollison but did not trouble the others. It was a woman's voice, from upstairs. Rollison glanced up to see Hindle's wife at one side of the landing leading to the staircase. She looked as meek and frail now as she had at Rubicon House, but what puzzled Rollison was the pair of field-glasses which dangled from her neck on to her flat chest.

"Arthur," she called, "I've finished."

"Have you seen anyone," called Hindle.

"No, dear. I'm absolutely sure no one's hiding anywhere within sight of the house. I'm sure I would have seen them. I've focused on every car and every tree, and if the house was surrounded I'd see some of the watchers, wouldn't I?"

"Yes, you'd see some of them," Hindle agreed, with deep satisfaction. "So you didn't bring the police, Rollison."

"I wouldn't want the police to know how deeply and in what way I was involved," Rollison pointed out.

Hindle cackled again, and even Derek grinned; and for the first time, both men lowered their guns. The woman looked down over the balustrade, the field-glasses dangling.

"What's been happening down there?" she called.

"Rollison's come to make a deal," explained Hindle. "Don't worry your head about it, Lou, just keep an eye on those windows."

"Where's the girl?" demanded Hindle's wife. "She picked the lock with a hairpin, the pin's still in the door. *I* couldn't help it," she added querulously. "I was making sure the house wasn't watched."

"It certainly wasn't your fault, Lou," said Hindle, soothingly. "You don't need to worry any more."

She said: "That's good, Arthur," and turned away.

Rollison continued to look upwards until he saw that she was no longer on the landing or the passages, so she must be in one of the rooms. The two Hindles were more relaxed than Rollison had yet seen them, Derek the more wary; Hindle himself gave the impression that he had rid himself of a great burden.

"I'll make a deal with you at seventy-five to us, twenty-five to you," he said; and sneered: "So this is how you make your money!"

"It's one way," Rollison answered. "I'll settle for one-third."

Derek said angrily: "There are three of us, as well as Ma."

"Derek," said his father, "the Toff can help us a great deal. He can smooth away a lot of difficulties, and I don't want any more argument. I'll settle for two-thirds, Rollison."

"That's good," Rollison said softly.

"How can we be sure he'll keep his word?" demanded Derek. "It will be a long time before Alec — " he nearly choked — "a long time before Tommy gets his money. How do we know we'll get our share?"

"That's just what I mean," said his father. "We'll have an agreement made out between us, and we'll have a tape recorder record, too. We'll have the Toff as tight as he's got us. He'll vouch for Alec being Tommy Loman, he'll help to get everything settled quickly with probate. How about that — a man with an unassailable reputation like the Toff won't have anything to worry about. It couldn't be better, Derek."

"He's not going to leave here until he's signed a confession," Derek insisted.

"We all sign one," Rollison interposed. "And we all put the same confession on tape, too. When we've all got copies we'll be able to trust each other." He slid his hand into his pocket and took out his cigarette case, selected a cigarette as if casually, but actually made sure it was one of those which contained a phial of tear gas. He put the cigarette to his lips and slid the case back into his pocket. "Why don't we get down to business?" He took out a book of matches, aware that Derek was watching every movement he made very closely, and laughed: "I still don't know how you fixed Alec George King. He threw me and the police off the scent."

"He's a friend of Derek," Hindle declared.

Rollison spun round, his expression changing on the instant: "He knows you! Why, he can give this away in five minutes!"

"Take it easy," Derek said, sneering. "He doesn't know me. I've supplied his pusher for a year or two, that's all."

"Pusher? Heroin?"

"Anything that comes," said Derek. "But it was too dangerous to go on with, and he couldn't find the dough so he had to do this deal. Don't worry about him or anyone."

Rollison put the cigarette to his lips and struck a match.

"There's just one person I worry about now."

"If you mean Effie — "

"I don't mean Effie," Rollison said. "I mean Tommy G. Loman. Is he alive or is he dead. When did you make the switch?" He smiled into Hindle's eyes. "Alec George King has done a wonderful job, he's fooled everybody except me, and if I hadn't realised he *was* King and not Loman, I would never have been able to make this deal. But for the record — where *is* he now?"

＊   ＊   ●

Outwardly, he looked so calm and self-possessed.

Inwardly, he was seething with anxiety, not only for himself, but for the real Tommy G. Loman.

Was he alive?

Or was he dead?

20

Switch In Time

THE TWO HINDLES stood silent.

The match burned low in Rollison's fingers and he shook it out, glanced about for an ashtray, and moved to one on a table against the wall. Hindle moved uneasily, and Derek said:

"Forget him."

"Don't be silly," said Rollison sharply. "I can't put all this through if the real Loman can appear out of the blue at any time."

"You said there were other ways to keep a man quiet than killing him," Hindle said.

"Not where Loman is concerned," Rollison replied sharply. "I want to see him, alive or dead." He laughed, without any humour. "That's an apt phrase in the circumstances. Wanted Thomas G. Loman, alive or dead, with a million pounds on his head. Where is he? Where was the switch made?"

"You're so clever, why don't you guess?" sneered Derek. "Pop, we don't tell Rollison anything else, he knows plenty. I'm not so sure he isn't bluffing, that we're not falling for a big confidence trick. I — "

He broke off, as a telephone bell rang.

Tension, eased until Rollison had switched the subject, demanding to see the real Thomas G. Loman, came screaming back. The harsh ringing of the bell made it worse. The elder Hindle raised the gun again as Derek moved towards a telephone standing on a table near a doorway on the right.

He said hoarsely: "Don't move, Rollison."

"Your son isn't safe to have around," Rollison said, the unlighted cigarette still in his mouth.

Derek reached the telephone and snatched up the receiver. Veins stood out on his forehead; so did blobs of sweat. He was so beside himself that he picked the receiver up while standing awkwardly to cover the Toff: for a moment the muzzle actually pointed at his own head.

"Yes?" he rasped; there was a moment's pause and he went on: "Yes, Alec?"

Alec.

Alec — Alec — Alec — Alec!

That was the moment when Rollison knew the whole truth; the moment he had fought for, staked his life on.

He had been as sure as he could be since Pamela had been attacked here that her companion had attacked her, not an unseen man. There had been time before her rescuers arrived; just time. Had they been half a minute later then her newfound lover would have choked her to death. He had felt certain that the man whom he had at first believed to be Thomas G. Loman was in fact Alec George King. And from the moment of realisation there had been only one concern in his mind: to find the real Thomas G.

Now, a man named Alec was on the telephone, knowing the Hindles were at the Browns' house.

Derek listened.

He twisted round, and his lips twisted in rare malevolence.

"Shoot him in the guts!" he cried. "He's conning us — one of Grice's men let it out, Alec heard them." Alec

George King, alias Thomas G. Loman, at Gresham Terrace. "He's conning — "

Rollison blew the phial of tear gas into Hindle's face before he realised what his son was saying. Derek twisted round, caught a wrist in the telephone cable, and jerked it free and levelled his gun, but before he touched the trigger Rollison used the small gun and a bullet caught the younger man in the shoulder. Derek grunted and jerked back, and Rollison shot him again with greater calculation, in the back of his gun hand.

Hindle was reeling about helplessly, hands at his streaming eyes.

Rollison listened intently but heard nothing upstairs. He picked up the telephone as the man named Alec called:

"Derek, what's happened? Are you there, are you there?"

Rollison simply rang off, and held the receiver down for a moment, then dialled 999 — the Emergency number. He was answered at once, and in seconds was speaking to Grice.

"Bill, there's a freelance newspaperman named Jack Fisher, attached to the construction side of London Airport. He was doing an inside story on a building strike when Tommy G. Loman's plane arrived. Find Fisher and I think you'll find the real Tommy G. Loman ... No, not the man at my flat, that's King ... The switch must have been made at London Airport and the real Tommy G. smuggled out through the new building work ... He might still be there, there are plenty of places to hide a man at London Airport."

He did not add: "And hide a body."

"What about you?" demanded Grice.

"I'm fine. The Browns are as innocent as doves, the Hindle family is here waiting for your chaps to come and pick them up. We may need an ambulance and we certainly need a doctor for the older Brown — he was thrown down the stairs."

Grice said: "Wait a moment." His voice faded and in the distance Rollison heard him say on another telephone: "London Airport Police, quickly . . ." Then in a louder voice he went on to Rollison: "I can't believe it. I can't believe the man at your flat isn't the *real* American."

"Brilliant act, isn't it?" asked Rollison.

"Brilliant. It — " There was another pause before Grice went on: "I'm going to take your word for it, but I still don't believe it. When — when did you begin to think —?" Grice broke off again, helplessly.

"There were a lot of indications, given hindsight," said Rollison, "but can't they keep? I want to tell Jolly, and get King himself. He is still at my flat, I take it?"

"No doubt at all," answered Grice. "Jolly was on the telephone only twenty minutes ago, and Loman himself — " Grice gulped — "I mean, King *alias* Loman picked up an extension and said: 'You find the Toff, do you hear? You find the Toff.' Yes," went on Grice, "he's there all right. Are you going straight to the flat?"

"As soon as I've tidied up here," Rollison said.

As he spoke, there was a rat-tat-tat at the front door; the first of three police cars had arrived. Rollison left the Hindles to them, told them about Mrs. Hindle, upstairs, and went to the cupboard beneath the stairs. The one thing above all others that he hated was the need to tell Pamela the truth about her Tommy, but at least the time was not yet.

"The police are in possession," he told her and her brother. "The Hindles are under arrest, and we know where to find King." He helped Pamela into the big hall, saying: "I had to discover where he was, and couldn't find the whole truth any other way."

"Richard," Pamela said. "I will never forgive myself for not trusting you." Then her tone changed. "How soon will a doctor be here for Daddy?"

"One's on the way," Rollison reassured her. "I don't think he broke any bones, and he's probably suffering from severe concussion."

"As soon as I know that for sure," Pamela said, "I want to go and see Tommy."

"Mr. Rollison!" a police sergeant called from the door.

Rollison had never been more glad of an interruption.

.   .   .

As he pulled up outside 25g Gresham Terrace, three-quarters of an hour later, Grice opened the door of a car which was double-parked and approached him. He might have news of Fisher as well as the real Tommy Loman. Rollison's heart pounded for the sake of a man whom he had never seen. But Grice was relaxed, and his stride was springy; he did not have the manner of a man bringing bad news.

"Alive?" asked Rollison.

"Alive." Grice stated, simply. "He was kept in an old hut on the building site. I'm pretty sure they were going to keep him alive until cement was being poured at the next section of the new terminal — they would have killed and buried him in double quick time. They kept him alive on bread and water, but he seems able to walk under his own steam. The switch was made with the connivance of a nurse, who was well paid. He's now at the airport hospital."

"Wonderful," Rollison breathed. "And Fisher?"

"He was picked up in Fleet Street," answered Grice. "He had one accomplice, another of the bomb throwing baskets. The moment he was arrested he began to blame Derek Hindle. He said Hindle forced him to do whatever he wanted by withholding heroin which he couldn't do without."

"Of them all Derek is undoubtedly the nastiest," Rollison said. They were half-way up the stairs then, and went the rest of the way in silence. The flat door opened, and Jolly came forward, eagerly, while Alec George King *alias* Thomas G. Loman peered from high above his head.

"Thank God you're all right, sir," Jolly said feelingly. "When you were so late back, without sending a message, I became very alarmed indeed."

"I'll say he did," confirmed 'Tommy'. "If you'd been much longer, Richard, you would have found him in bed in a state of collapse. Where have you been, partner?"

"At the Browns' house," Rollison answered, mildly.

'Tommy' stared.

Then he gulped, and backed a pace.

Then he dropped his right hand to his pocket, but before he could pull it out again Rollison covered him with the small gun. Jolly simply gaped. Grice made a swift movement, drawing a pair of handcuffs from his pocket, while Rollison lifted a stiletto from 'Tommy's' — one of the weapons from the Trophy Wall. There were moments of almost screaming tension, before Alec George King *alias* Tommy G. Loman asked in a husky voice quite free from American accent:

"How did you guess?"

"Too many police were at the Browns' house when you took Pamela home for any one to have attacked her and got away. It had to be you. The only prisoner caught was Luigi Tetano, a policeman from Long Island, and the only other man about was you. Would you have choked the life out of Pamela if the police hadn't been there, I wonder?"

King managed to retort: "I wonder."

"Once I realised you were the wrong Tommy I saw

all the other indications. That nothing fitted if you were the real man, everything did if you were not. That your reaction to London was too naive for anyone from the far west, you *had* to be putting on an act. You were prepared to stay here, snug and safe, although the man you pretended to be would never have stayed. As I told the Superintendent, it is easy with hindsight."

"Clever Toff," King half-sneered. "I thought I'd got away with it."

"I can hardly believe all this," Jolly said, in a hollow voice. "When — when was the switch made, sir?"

"Oh, in the airport hospital," Rollison said. "That one's easy." He explained about the nurse, and then added: "The ward was left empty two or three times, the new extension was being built behind a canvas and plastic screen. It was very simple. In fact it was all beautifully simple — even Jack Fisher arriving on the scene to find out what Pamela had told me, and to ingratiate himself so that he could come to the flat and keep the false Tommy up to date with what was happening."

There were so many more details, among them that Loman's baggage had been stolen so that Alec George King could have all his identification papers and his clothes and credits. That Alec had known of Tetano's identity because Fisher had picked up the news from London Airport police.

Later that day the police learned that the Hindles, once on the run, simply took over the Browns' house. They had feared the Toff most, and Pamela next, because sooner or later they might have discovered the truth about 'Tommy'. And Alec George King had made his fierce, overwhelming conquest to find out what she knew. He would not have killed her, he swore, simply overpowered her and taken her into the house where her father and brother were held captive.

Later that evening, too, Rollison went to see Pamela Brown.

She had been kept at the house by the police, she said with great indignation; or she would have been at Gresham Terrace on their heels. And, with fresh indignation, she demanded of Rollison:

"Why isn't he here with you? Why didn't you bring him?"

"Pamela," Rollison said as he put his hand on her arm and led her into the hall where a few hours ago he had been so near death, "try not to hate me."

"Hate *you*? Why on earth should I?"

"For what I have to tell you," Rollison said.

Her eyes were so huge and bright but they held no radiance. Her lips were parted, but she uttered no words although three words formed on them, easy to read:

"He's — not — dead?"

"No," Rollison told her, "he's not dead, Pam, but I think perhaps he deserves to be."

Gently, he told her.

He did not know whether it was good or bad that she listened, and made no comment, and showed no sign of tears.

When he had done, and waited a while, Rollison went on: "There's one deep cause for satisfaction, Pamela. You and your family did what you set out to do: you saved the life and fortune of the real Tommy G. Loman."

■   ■   ■

When he saw that real Tommy G., the next day, he found him pleasant and likeable. But Rollison knew and Jolly knew and Pamela would soon know that as a personality he wasn't a patch on the false Tommy G. Loman: and never would be.